THE IMAGE IN MY MIND

PETER KENNEDY

Copyright © PETER KENNEDY 2020
This book is sold subject to the condition that it shall not, by way of trade or otherwise, be lent, resold, hired out, or otherwise circulated without the publisher's prior consent in any form of binding or cover other than that in which it is published and without a similar condition including this condition being imposed on the subsequent publisher.
The moral right of PETER KENNEDY has been asserted.
ISBN-13: 9798667149392

This is a work of fiction. Names, characters, businesses, organizations, places, events and incidents either are the product of the author's imagination or are used fictitiously. Any resemblance to actual persons, living or dead, events, or locales is entirely coincidental.

For Marek Dominiczak

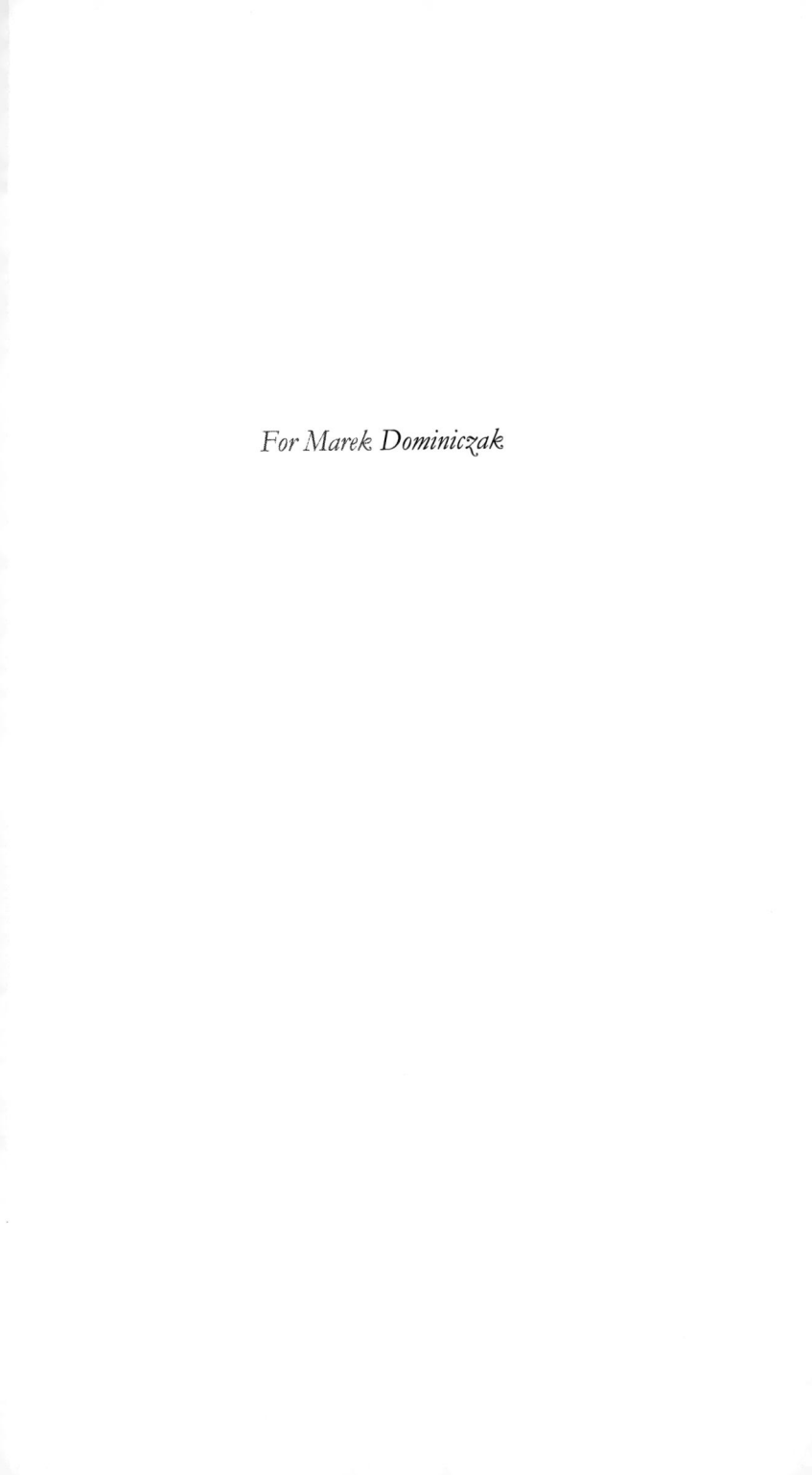

CONTENTS

I 1
II 21
III 33
IV 44
V 59
VI 71
VII 85
ABOUT THE AUTHOR 106

I

DORSET MAY 2017

By any standards, Doctor Roger Cosgrove is a complex network of human contradictions. Everything about him is as confusing to an observer as it is to himself. He is both an authentic rebel in spirit and an obedient and compliant citizen in his everyday actions. His views are extremely liberal in some areas yet clearly conservative in others. He believes passionately in the inalienable rights of the individual in society yet he also endorses the principle of a nation's collective responsibility and the rule of law. While he has contempt for almost all politicians, on both sides of the chamber, most of whom he usually loathes, both because of their trademark dissembling and the fact that they never seem to answer the questions put to them by interviewers, nevertheless he thoroughly supports the legitimacy of an elected parliament that has a mandate to govern the country and make laws. While he believes in the intrinsic stability and value of the standard family unit, nevertheless he is unquestionably a true liberal in his non-judgemental approach to the sexual peccadillos of everyone else, including some of his academic colleagues who seem to him to be particularly adept at this form of human behaviour. He is highly sceptical of everything he reads in scientific journals and newspapers, most of which he is entirely convinced is either wrong, inaccurate or both, but at the same time he has an intrinsic, if not surprising, respect for the truthfulness and integrity of the printed article. He is extremely cynical about both the motivation and professionalism of the medical profession, especially following his late wife's recent demise in hospital, yet he shows great respect for any healthcare professional he encounters in everyday life and discourse. While he is ruthlessly parsimonious in relation to his own needs, he is by contrast exceptionally generous financially to his family and friends. While he has a deep suspicion, bordering on hate in some cases, of individual people he comes across both in the workplace and elsewhere, he also has a profound respect and feeling for the collective notion of humankind.

So the question to be answered is whether Roger is just an intensely human man, one imbued with a profound sense of natural honesty, or whether he is just a very difficult and cantankerous misanthrope. Or to put it more bluntly, a few unkind and ungenerous people might call him a bitter and miserable old bastard. To add to this intrinsic confusion, perhaps he has elements of both. But surely that would make him very human indeed, wouldn't you say? Now, that really is a tough one to be sure about. Anyway, he may be quite a difficult person but there is unquestionably a good deal of empathetic humanity and compassion coursing through Roger's veins, and he has the capacity to be both hard and soft many times a day. So he is indeed a most genuine contradiction if nothing else.

But there is little contradiction when it comes to his deep emotions. As he looks out of the large bay window of his small and relatively isolated cottage, within ten minutes walking distance of Weymouth, his thoughts inevitably coalesce around the memories of his late wife Caroline. With the pale grey curtains fully drawn back, he has a panoramic view of nature at its most enigmatic and splendid, with an untainted azure blue sky far above, beneath which there are asymmetric rows of tall poplar and oak trees lining the gravel path on either side, all the way to the main road leading eventually to the town of Weymouth and the Isle of Portland further south. Scattered here and there throughout the vista, he thinks he can spot a few orange and red pine trees with their needle-like leaves. He's almost sure that just behind the large tree formations there are also a few rhododendron shrubs, displaying their impressive red, pink and white flowers. How they both loved being amongst those colourful spring wonders. A few hundred metres farther along the road he knows he will get a fine view of Portland Harbour and the Sailing Academy. For a moment he feels a sense of strange regret that they had never even tried that particular sport, yet that would hardly have been an easy thing to arrange when they had lived most of their lives in the fine city of Edinburgh. But perhaps he is just trying to justify what was really a lack of motivation rather than a real lack of opportunity. Anyway, as far as he is concerned, that thought no longer has any meaning.

Caroline, the one and only true love of his life, died of ovarian cancer exactly eighteen months previously, and painfully so in more ways than one. They had been married for thirty- one years and had been unusually happy together. It all seemed so innocent at first, just a bit of stomach bloating and discomfort, but when she started to lose weight without trying it was clear to both of them that something very sinister was lurking in her body. He'd willingly paid for a private consultation with a gynaecology specialist because they weren't prepared to wait several weeks for an NHS appointment and the woman their general practitioner recommended had a fine reputation. It only took three days to establish the diagnosis of a malignant primary cancer in her right ovary, and further tests showed that it had already spread widely in her slender body, invading the lungs, liver and who knows what else besides. Caroline was a brave woman and decided she wanted to enjoy her remaining few months of life, something that would not have been at all likely after several rounds of chemotherapy.

She endured the first infusion of cancer-killing drugs but then called things to a halt. Given just a few months to live, which might well have been extended slightly by chemotherapy, she made a conscious and informed decision not to have any treatment except painkillers. Roger and she then spent the next three months travelling to beauty spots in Scotland and Northern England and going to as many art galleries and classical concerts as possible. Soon after that she was just too ill and in too much pain to travel anywhere or to do almost anything and she opted to undergo palliative care in a hospice in Edinburgh where she was very well cared for. While she had not worked officially as an English teacher for several years, he still had his job as an information technology (IT) expert; his primary position was as a well-respected Reader at the local university while he also had a very strong link with industry.

His employers were more than considerate and generous to him in view of his awful situation and he was given a great deal of compassionate leave.

Despite this generosity of spirit, Caroline died peacefully in the hospice, loaded to the gills with morphine and loved to the very last minute by Roger, and also, he was sure, by most of the hospice staff caring for her. He had never known anyone to show such dignity and courage at the end of their life. The whole thing from diagnosis to death was four and a half months and she was only fifty-six, a mere six years younger than he. The end came with uncivilised speed. A very good looking woman with beautiful clear blue eyes, and thick auburn hair with the occasional grey streak, she had always appeared remarkably youthful. It was almost macabre that she retained her young looks right until the very end. Perhaps that was nature's cruel little joke.

However awful her illness and death may have been for him, their two children, Michael and Adrian, also suffered hideously over the death of their mother. Both boys were single and in good jobs, and their overwhelming emotion had been one of abject loss and a strong sense that it was all so incredibly unfair. Unfortunately, as any medical specialist will tell you, fatal illnesses have a recurrent tendency to be both random and profoundly unfair. A sense of fairness just doesn't come into the equation of life and death. It may have been easier for Roger to bear had he possessed some kind of religious faith but he was a confirmed humanist with not even the slightest belief in God or an afterlife. How he desperately envied true believers in these things after Caroline died, greatly deluded as they might be or so it seemed to him. The end result was a great deal of anger on his part, which only added to his already angry demeanour, as well as an understandable depression at what had happened and his new-found loneliness, and a complete cessation of interest in either his career or his specialist interest in computers and artificial intelligence. In a way, this was a double pity as his University head of department was just about to recommend his promotion to a full professorship, one that had frankly been long overdue for a solid academic of his intellectual stature who was already sixty-two years old. The truth is that Roger just didn't care about anything after this tragedy, and two months after her death he took early retirement and severed all academic links with both his university and industry.

At one time, he had been hugely ambitious for his academic career, but that rather selfish enthusiasm was now a thing of the past and quickly lost its seductive allure after the cruel destruction of his family life. In retrospect, retirement was probably not a very sensible decision but he was insistent about it even when the benign and fatherly (though younger than he) head of department did his level best to dissuade him from what he thought was probably an unwise reflex and precipitate course of action. But Roger's mind was made up and nothing anyone could say, including his children's pleas, could make him change his mind. To make a complete break of it, he also decided to move house and sold his four-bedroom town house in Edinburgh for a tidy sum and bought a small but stylish cottage, slightly off the beaten track, in Weymouth which was a town that held a particularly special place in both their hearts. He was sure Caroline would have been happy for him to have moved there and the truth is that his grief was so great that he just needed to completely change his surroundings, much as he knew he would miss the cultural richness and diversity of Edinburgh. In the year that he had been living in this region of Dorset, with its inspiring and exquisite countryside, close proximity to the sea, and historical link to the birthplace and novels of Thomas Hardy, one of his favourite writers, Roger had not regretted his decision to relocate even for a minute. Whether he really believed that or whether it was more a question of self-justification of his actions, no one – not even he – could fathom. Perhaps it was a bit of both.

Whether he likes it or not – and even he isn't sure what he feels – Roger is now isolated in his cosy little cottage and entirely alone in the world. He feels that his home has great character despite its size, and as he moves from room to room (of which there are not many), he has a strange feeling that it is a kind of palimpsest of everything that characterised its previous owners. However, despite this, he has no sense of it being haunted. For the present, that is enough for him and what he feels he wants. Time really is the great healer of wounds, though it is sometimes also the cause of them – the so-called time wound. There are certainly some friendly faces in the nearby townships and a few people living near him have become aware of his tragic personal history. He manages to give an agreeable grunt or wave to some of his more affable neighbours when he passes them on the pathways or streets, but in reality he hardly gives anyone a real chance to get to know him or show their more friendly and charitable side. In a word, he has chosen to wallow in his own personalised misery, and that is never a wise thing to do however fate has treated you.

His two adult sons live in different apartments in the outer suburbs of the capital city of London, and he has only seen them on three occasions over the last year. He also has occasional phone calls and Zoom contact with them – he is an IT expert after all – and has also been visited twice by his two closest friends and their wives, but on the whole he has chosen to live the life of a modern hermit. He keeps himself in relatively good physical condition by walking a few miles every day along either the broad esplanade adjoining Weymouth's impressive sandy beach. If he is feeling more adventurous, he might walk all the way to Portland and admire the flotillas of sailing ships in the harbour along the way and then on occasion take in the graduated contours of the pebbly Chesil Beach. It is a real pity that he has no interest whatsoever in palaeontology as his home and stomping grounds are in direct juxtaposition to the Jurassic Coast which is a veritable gold mine for fossil hunters. While he and Caroline had once visited the famous Nothe Fort, with its impressive, if rather frightening, World War II fortifications, and experienced first-hand what may possibly have been a haunted corridor in its basement, they had never got as far as Portland Prison and he has no intention of going there without her. Despite his daily routine, which certainly imbues him with a formal sense of normality, he has never truly recovered from his personal loss, and, if he is honest with himself, he probably never will. Nor is that something he particularly wants to happen. Such is the relentless and unforgiving nature of grief, especially when manifest in as troubled a soul as Roger.

Having a solid structure to one's day is often the key to keeping a hold on sanity, or at least for maintaining some semblance of a normal life. He may have functioned outside the box, so to speak, in his academic world, but in the realm of everyday living Roger is a realist and from the outset in his new home and with his altered lifestyle he created a fairly rigid structure to his day. He did this in the hope and expectation that he wouldn't fall into the all-too-frequent abyss of severe boredom and the resulting *ennui,* the two mental states he fears more than any other. But it was also important for him not to sink aimlessly into a kind of rut, and become profoundly boring even to himself, so within this daily framework he tries hard to inject elements of originality and spontaneity from time to time. But that's not so easily done if you are grieving or depressed or, as is the case with him, both. Anyway, he aims to vary his routine at least once per week, but he never decides in advance which particular day of the week it will be. He still retains a few selected elements of wisdom if that is not a contradiction in terms.

Every morning at around ten he goes for his main walk of the day, a one-hour round trip to the charming and picturesque Weymouth town with its pristine sandy beach and benign seafront which seems to provide a sort of tolerant haven for so many elderly and frail people. The pretty harbour has an abundance of private boats that he could never hope to afford on his University pension, and a magisterial esplanade with its elegant architecture and Georgian terraces. When the historic town bridge is elevated to let tall ships pass he just has to wait and spend longer outside, though it must be said that his sense of genuine awe at this architectural anachronism more than makes up for any delay it might cause. No wonder King George III had such an affinity for the place. Roger could have chosen just about anywhere to relocate (apart from the ultra-expensive London where he was actually brought up and which he now rather dislikes for all sorts of reasons), but he somehow landed in Dorset and doesn't pine for Scotland. Sometimes he feels a trifle isolated but that negative feeling seldom lasts for very long, and the advantages of his new home and life more than compensate for any of its perceived social or cultural shortcomings. The fact that the Black Death first came to this town in the fourteenth century impresses him more with a charming sense of history than any modicum of vicarious horror. There is for sure not a scintilla of snobbery lurking anywhere in his being. That is true, unless of course you count a curious sense of inverse snobbery as a real feeling.

It was on just such a day as this, as he was enjoying walking in a bracing May morning that seemed to energise his entire spirit, when a train of events was set in motion that managed to change his entire perception of the world and also, perhaps rather sadly, impede his growing sense of self-confidence and nascent emergence from grief. But life is always so unpredictable. Otherwise it wouldn't be life as we know it. That is both the problem and the point.

When he returned from his regular morning walk that day, May 16th (he always remembers it was on a Tuesday), he noticed a large brown jiffy bag that had been left by the postman just in front of the pale green front door of his cottage. He bent down to pick it up and saw it was clearly much too wide to be shoved through the narrow letter box in the door so it was not a particular surprise to find it where it was. It was addressed in neat capital ink handwriting to 'Dr Roger Cosgrove PhD' so there was no question it was meant for him. He opened the front door with his regular key, the one attached to a small silver elephant keyring that Caroline had given him as a present ten years before, and entered the cottage with the envelope neatly tucked under his right arm. At this stage he had absolutely no idea what it was though he was sure he recognised his younger son's handwriting on the envelope even though it was in capitals. He thinks he knows young Adrian better than he actually does. Perhaps it's the other way round.

For some reason he can't quite fathom, Roger does not open the package immediately after he's placed it on the kitchen table. He has this strange, almost intangible, feeling that what the package contains is not entirely benign. So before he touches it again he makes a particularly good cappuccino using his expensive espresso coffee machine and observes the object closely while he slowly drinks, savouring the rich aroma and powerful taste as he sips and then slowly swallows the smooth brown liquid. But after a few minutes, curiosity gets the better of him and he tears open the jiffy bag, an action requiring considerable skill as the top end is sealed with strong duct tape. After about half a minute of focused pulling and tearing, he opens the package and as he does so he thinks he hears a high-pitched cry, most likely human, but he isn't quite sure and dismisses this as an irrelevant delusion. The object he withdraws from the packaging is itself wrapped in several layers of brown tissue paper which adds both bulk and weight to the package he first picked up. *That makes sense,'* he thinks to himself.

Just for a second, he pauses as the wild thought that the parcel could be a bomb enters and almost immediately evaporates from his mind, but after dismissing this fear as quite absurd, he continues unwrapping the rest of the package. Besides, he reasons, no one in their right mind would send a bomb to him. But who in their right mind would even consider doing such a thing? The answer begs the question. At the centre of the parcel he finds two objects stuck together. One is clearly a DVD placed snugly inside a much larger plastic wallet. The other is an envelope addressed to him with his name neatly written in what he is sure is his son Adrian's handwriting with its clear slightly forward sloping but eminently readable scrawl. It's interesting to see that style, which is thought by some graphologists to indicate an optimistic demeanour (which is certainly the case), whereas Roger's writing is messy and scarcely legible and slopes backwards, indicating more of a pessimistic nature, something that is definitely true as well. For a rational man of science he is, clearly, more than capable of acting on and believing in notions that don't have a solid scientific foundation to say the least. But in his experience, that also goes for most of his colleagues and probably just about everyone else. We all pretend to be rational, but in reality none of us are.

He detaches the envelope from the DVD and opens it with his right thumb. He removes a letter which had been placed inside and begins to read its handwritten message carefully. He soon feels a strong sense of relief though it isn't altogether clear why he was so anxious in the first place. Was he meant to be anxious? The letter is from Adrian and is both unsurprising and self-explanatory.

Dear Dad,

I hope you are keeping well and enjoying village life, the sea and the Dorset countryside (as far as you can without mum of course). I'm OK here and so is Michael. I think he and Susan are getting closer all the time, so who knows? You may have a daughter-in-law before you think!

So anyway, I was going through all my things hoping to find a lot of junk to throw away and make this place where I'm living a bit tidier (that will be the day!) when I found five old-fashioned film reels of you and your family in the 1960s and 1970s, presumably taken with your father's cine-camera. I don't know what camera grandpa used but presumably it was a 35 mm film for making home movies. Anyway I took these film rolls to a local photographer and the very smart guy in charge converted all of them into a DVD format (he said it was easy – clever bloke!), and joined them all up into just one big home movie. Judging by the original dates written on the film reel covers, it covers the periods when I guess you must have been about eight, ten, thirteen, fifteen and seventeen years old. Very interesting and I was amazed at the physical resemblance between you and me – genetics I guess but still pretty striking. It was also quite weird to see Uncle Peter as a boy – he looks nothing like you and was of course four years older. Four of these movies were taken on your summer holidays and one was clearly a cine record of your bar mitzvah so for that one you must have been thirteen (a man already!). God, that one is absolutely hilarious and also a bit sad in a way. It was obviously very sad as well to see your sister Margaret in the first two reels and I really hope that doesn't make you too upset though I realise it probably will. Still, if nothing else these are a kind of living record of your childhood and what the earth looked like around fifty years ago.

So I thought I should send them to you as a gift (though I know it's not your birthday yet) and I really hope you get something out of them, though perhaps not any real joy at the moment. Some of the images are a bit misty and grainy but this was after all before the digital revolution (didn't you write a review paper on that some time ago?).

I'm looking forward to seeing you again soon and do phone me (you have my mobile number as I almost never use my landline any more) after you have seen them all to let me know what you think.

Love Adrian xx

Roger re-reads the letter several times before he is able to take in what it means and all the implications. His sister Margaret was killed in a road traffic accident when she was fourteen years old in 1966. They had been very close, though she was two years older than he, and he knows that his parents, who are now both dead, never fully recovered from the sudden shock of her death and their prolonged grief. He remembers his mother telling him that this was the only occasion when she ever saw her husband openly weeping. These days this would be regarded as completely normal but at that time, fifty years ago, such open displays of raw emotion were rather frowned upon. He thinks that was one of the worst aspects of his childhood, along with the widespread, but often unspoken, racism which he hated, and still hates, with a vengeance. But he is proud of his two sons and Adrian has always been such a sweet-natured and thoughtful boy. *'Just like his mother,'* he thinks to himself.

That evening, after finishing off the remains of a microwaved and rather tasteless chicken casserole followed by his favourite desert – vanilla ice cream with chocolate sauce – he goes for his trademark forty-minute early evening walk up to the Weymouth sea front, and soon afterwards makes himself comfortable in his recently upholstered armchair in the cottage's small but cosy living room. Suitably but not entirely satiated in most areas, he then decides to have a quick look at the DVD his son has sent him. He inserts the innocent-looking disc into the side of his TV/DVD player and waits to be entertained, with that rather impatient feeling most people get just before a film comes on screen, when the image of the electronically signed rating certificate invariably irritates people rather than entertaining them – a necessary prerequisite to the main feature and evidence that people much wiser than you have given the film its formal status. Instead of a rating certificate, he sees a colour picture with large blue lettering proclaiming it is 'My Holiday' rather than some kind of feature film, and within a few seconds he sees a grainy series of lines and flashes in yellow and white before the clearer image of the mighty Swiss Alps suddenly fills the screen. The initial picture shows a series of rugged grey snow-capped mountains punctuated by broad areas of green trees and grass that seem to separate them and reach all the way up to their bases. In the foreground he recognises a rather thin boy about eight years old with an anxious, yet quizzical, expression, holding his mother's hand and in the distance in front of them he can just about see curiously blurred images of his older brother Peter and also his sister Margaret who together are trundling down a gravel pathway. Then more flashes and lines appear in yellow before the picture becomes clearer again. So far he sees nothing much to surprise him. The cine camera was handheld so the images are jerky which after a while becomes increasingly tiring for the eyes. He fast forwards to the next reel and sees the same figures but slightly older and in a seaside setting very different from the magnificent vistas reproduced before. So clearly, the original primitive reels have been converted in sequence, each one named in large black letters before it starts, as his tidy organised mind would have expected.

At this point he makes a decision, one which is to have significant consequences for his mental state, already far more fragile than either he or his few friends and remaining family realise. He decides to spend about twenty minutes every evening watching one film reel, representing a particular time point in his childhood, and hopes that in some way this might both entertain him a little while also allowing him to put the past into some kind of perspective. Right now he feels very strongly that's what he needs. The whole project will last no longer than a week. Anyway, that was the general idea. The problem with ideas is that unless you are particularly lucky they seldom gel with what is truly real in the world.

II

The following evening marked the start of Roger's new experience, or at least that's how he chose to see it. At that early stage he simply thought of viewing old home movies as a welcome distraction from his usual routine, one that certainly did not have the slightest element of risk. The fact that the quality of the images was primitive by his own ultra-modern IT standards didn't faze him at all. Quite the contrary – he thought of the whole thing as rather quaint, in fact a re-enacted past memory that he was able to view in the present. It was nothing more than that. He was right at least in reasoning that there was no physical risk.

He'd decided in advance to look carefully at just the first reel that evening, the one shot by his late father in what must have been the summer of 1962 when the whole family, or at least as it was then, was based for their holiday in the region of Lake Como in Northern Italy. Though he knows he was a rather precocious eight-year-old boy at the time, he has only vague and subliminal memories of the trip though he does have a hazy recollection of his father driving through the spectacular Maloja Pass in the Swiss Alps connecting Switzerland with the Lombardy region of Italy. This was the quickest and certainly the most scenic route to reach their final destination which was a pleasant three-star hotel along the banks of the beautiful Lake Como where they were to stay for two weeks. Though his short-term memory for recent events is only slightly above average, he has a phenomenal long-term memory and can remember events in his distant past with exceptional precision.

One day, he thinks to himself, clever neuroscientists will discover the biological basis of memory, something he doubts will ever emerge from advances in his own specialist field of artificial intelligence. But of course he could be wrong about that, and he has a rather endearing tendency to doubt almost everything he thinks. He can still just about recall the magnificence of the winding road, the magisterial vistas the four passengers were feasting their eyes on, and the sheer drops on the side of the forbidding but beautiful mountains, chasms that clearly terrified his long-suffering parents who were very much products of the War generation. Despite the six years of terror and hell they had both experienced, particularly during the Blitz, they were still easily frightened, especially of authority – both man-made and the unfeeling consequences of natural events which were inevitably unpredictable. Perhaps their innate sense of fear was all about a lack of control. Maybe that is also Roger's own main problem. But, if it is, then it must be just one of a multitude of problems and hang-ups that have bedevilled his sixty-three years on the planet.

The first few minutes of the film are already familiar to him from his viewing of the previous evening. He recognises the imposing mountain scenery in the background under a vast blue skyline, and reckons the family must have taken a break from what must have been a pretty relentless and hazardous drive through the winding ascending and then descending roads of the Maloja Pass. Never one to tolerate heights, Roger feels slightly dizzy just looking at the sheer drops along the sides of the mountains shown in the picture frames and imagining what it must have been like. In fact he's pretty sure he was very scared of the heights and dangers at the time. That much certainly hasn't changed since then. No wonder his father, usually a rather mild-mannered man, became so anxious and irritable on these exhilarating but terrifying journeys. It must have been quite a sense of responsibility and a stressful ordeal for the poor man. His equally frightened mother frequently waved a small bottle of smelling salts under her husband's nose in a vain attempt to keep him alert. But his father didn't need a wake-up call to maintain his fear of sudden automobile disaster. The fact that he had an automatic car made the descent even more hazardous than normal because of the ever-present danger of the brakes burning out. And that did happen on one occasion. No pleasure ever comes without due payment.

Then quite suddenly the picture focuses on his sister Margaret who is staring at the camera, smiling broadly with all the subtle innocence of a ten-year-old child. Of course no one thought for one second that she would be killed four years later, and certainly not her, a vivacious and sensitive young girl whom he had adored for her kindness to him, her sense of joy, and her wisdom that was somehow beyond her years. As he caught a historical glimpse of her curly brown hair and enormous blue eyes he became aware of a deep sense of loss that he'd not felt for decades. Clearly this jerky movie with all its quaint echoes of amateurism was more than able to reach the parts of his troubled psyche that had long lain dormant, or at least so he thought. There were no images on this reel of his father since he must have been the only cameraman, but his mother is in some scenes. While both his parents had seemed to him as old as Methuselah at the time, in reality they were probably both only in their late thirties, an age that seems irritatingly young to him now. She was plumper and plainer than she became a few years later, but this may well have reflected the lingering effects of post-war austerity. It was only later that she became a glamorous woman, presumably because she took her appearance more seriously and dressed herself more sumptuously when the family became a little richer and the prevailing ethos of the 1960s put subtle pressure on people to appear more physically attractive. His older and cleverer brother Peter always hated being filmed so it was no surprise that he only appeared, in this reel at least, in the distance and usually running away.

Then he sees himself, an embryonic form of what he would eventually become. Roger does not feel any sense of pride or pleasure at the vision of this seemingly detached child, who is seen half smiling self-consciously as he chews a sweet (possibly a wine gum) while simultaneously holding his mother's hand as they both carefully negotiate the rocky pathway that must have been several hundred yards from the veteran Vauxhall Cresta, a family car that he remembers was almost laughably ahead of its time in its smooth aerodynamic design. Now it would be a vintage prize for some obsessional motor head. How fashion changes. But what really catches Roger's attention is the intense look his childhood self gives to the camera, one that is quite uncanny as it's somehow both naïve and insightful in a way that only children can master. He can't get away from a chilling feeling that his very younger self is either judging him or else trying to give him a warning. But a warning about what? At first he dismisses this feeling as completely absurd, but he then remembers the cry he'd heard the day before as he was opening the parcel. Was that real or, infinitely more likely, did he just imagine it or misinterpret some other extraneous sound? Roger is an intensely rational man, a true scientist, one who generally only believes something to be true when he sees clear unequivocal evidence that it is indeed the case. But he also believes that if there is the remotest possibility that something could be true, even if it is a chance in ten million, then given sufficient time, which could of course be aeons, then even the most unlikely possibility will ultimately turn out to be true. So, on that basis, for something to be completely dismissed as untrue or a fantasy, he has to be one hundred per cent certain that it could never be true. How can anyone be that sure of anything in this world? He doesn't know the answer to that which means, logically, that just about anything, no matter how bizarre, could potentially be true. And that includes ghosts, the supernatural and the existence of God. He remembers one of his very religious friends at school, a rather pale, earnest and charming young man with a mass of ginger hair and a face almost completely adorned with spots of every shape and shade, telling him that not everything in the world is either known or can be explained by science. Well he certainly had a point, he reckons, but a rational being must still live according to the evidence that presents itself all around us. How else can one live one's life without going mad, literally confused by the labour of one's own thinking, and also so obsessed by constant doubts about everything in the world that everyday life becomes just about impossible? With these rather sobering thoughts in mind, Roger finished looking at that first twenty-minute film reel and then decided to listen to some of his favourite classical music on his iPod to clear his mind and discard unhelpful notions. He looked forward, more than usual, to going to sleep that night.

His optimism for a peaceful night turned out to be both premature and misplaced. No one has yet worked out the true function of dreaming. Some people have suggested that dreams allow the brain to process and somehow make some kind of sense of the mass of information and external input that enters the brain during the day. Others are certain that some of their best ideas are conceived during dreaming, while the pioneer psychoanalyst Sigmund Freud thought that dreams were essentially wish fulfilments. In other words, we are all still completely in the dark on this enigmatic issue. As far as Roger is concerned, dreaming is just something that happens to all of us during sleep which perhaps scientists will understand one day, though as an artificial intelligence expert, he has always thought that we won't understand the true function, if any, of dreams until we fully understand the fundamental basis of consciousness itself. He doesn't regard this rather pessimistic view as being in the least bit nihilistic. He sees it as realistic as it will probably take up to a hundred years to determine the biological basis of self-awareness and consciousness – the 'holy grail' of neuroscience. In the scientific sense, he is probably right. But in the spiritual sense, he is probably wrong. It all depends.

We know that people dream during periods of rapid eye movement (REM) sleep, in which the eyes are moving haphazardly in all different directions for about fifteen minutes, and that these periods occur roughly five times per night. These REM periods tend to be more prolonged as the period of sleep progresses. That evening, Roger went through his usual night-time routine consisting of an invigorating hot shower followed by a quick clean of is teeth with his electric toothbrush before laying his head down to sleep for the night in his luxurious double bed. While an innately frugal man, Roger is certainly no masochist and doesn't wear a hair shirt against his bare skin. He still likes his little pleasures and sleeping well is certainly one of them. But when he woke up frightened and in a cold sweat at three o'clock in the morning he was able to recall all the details of the dream, or, perhaps more accurately, the nightmare, he had just experienced with considerable clarity. That is unusual, as in general the details of even a nightmare have a distinct tendency to evaporate before they can be remembered clearly. In the dream, he had a brief but disconcerting conversation with his eight-year-old former self who had seemed to stare at him so intensely across the mysterious time divide from the home movie.

In his dream, he again found himself in the rocky valley looking at the mighty Swiss Alps in the distance, but the key difference was that he was actually in among the family and the picturesque landscape, and not just an observer of the past. While he somehow knew he was within a dream, presumably his own, for some obscure reason he had no desire to wake himself up. He felt a curious sense of detachment but, unexpectedly, not an iota of fear.

He sat down on a nearby rock with a flattened surface that was jutting out of the ground and was soon confronted by the eight-year-old boy who did not sit down but stood still and firm with both his arms akimbo. Though he knew he was about to converse with himself, albeit at a much younger age, nevertheless he perceived the boy as being an entirely separate human entity. It was a strange experience, and certainly surreal, but he knew somehow that it wasn't truly real except perhaps in his own mind, though not his imagination as such.

The boy stepped right up to him and stared hard with his limpid blue eyes.

'Hello Roger,' he said quietly to the boy.

The boy looked at him again with that off-putting quizzical look before speaking.

'Do I know you?'

'Well I think you should,' he replied.

'Mummy and daddy told me never to speak to strangers so it's naughty for me to be speaking to you now.'

Roger was taken aback though he fully understood why this warning had been given. He remembers having been told this by his parents many years before.

'You don't have to worry about me. I'm not a bad person and I'm not a threat to you. I just want to talk. I won't harm you. You can call your parents over here if you want.'

'No, they can hear me if I shout or scream.'

'Of course they can.'

'What did you want to tell me mister?' 'Do you have any idea who I am?'

'Not really,' was the unsure reply.

'Not really? Does that mean a sort of yes?'

The boy stared at Roger again, this time even harder. He could never remember being able to stare at anyone for such a long period without laughing or just averting his eyes.

'Yes sort of.'

'Right,' he replied.

A hiatus during which neither spoke a word followed for about fifteen seconds. The boy was the first to break the silence.

'Yes I think I know who you are.'

'Good, so who am I then?'

'You're me aren't you?'

'Well done, you got it in one.'

'One what?' asked the boy.

'What I mean is that you're right. I am what you will become in the future.'

'You mean not now?'

'Yes that's right, not now.'

The boy suddenly looked startled, but not scared, and spoke again.

'You have to be careful, Roger.'

'But careful of what Roger?'

'Be careful. You are in danger. You might die quite soon.'

He was surprised but not fazed by this.

'Roger, when you get to my age you can die at any time.'

'I didn't mean at your age. You might die before you're as old as you are.'

'I don't quite understand what you mean. I'm alive now.'

'Are you?' the boy asked.

At that point the boy smiled, gave a childish mock salute and walked away briskly down to a rocky overhang about a hundred yards away where the rest of his family had gathered.

At that point, Roger woke up and he remembers nothing more about the dream. He was certainly a bit disturbed by its contents, and was now sweating, but he was not unduly concerned. Maybe he should have been. After a few anxious minutes of recollection, he went back to sleep. This time he didn't dream at all.

III

He loves the season of spring above all the others. A typically beautiful May morning with a cloudless, bright blue sky high above and window-filtered sunlight of almost Arcadian clarity greeted Roger the next day and wrapped itself around him with a bracing but benign vitality. As he prepared and then quickly ate his modest breakfast, the one that hardly ever varies, he felt able to consign the still vivid memory of the previous night's dream to the lees of insignificant imagination, something more akin to the nonsensical processes of the unconscious brain. For sure, he still felt a mild sense of unease, but he could deal with that, especially when surrounded on all sides by life's energising reality and promised pleasures. That day, he looked forward to his morning walk with unusual anticipation. But he is not a complete automaton and is still able to inject a modicum of variation into his tried and tested exercise regime, one that has also proved to be more than beneficial for his somewhat battered soul.

He decides on this occasion to walk along the graduated pebble shoreline of Chesil Beach, an area that particularly appeals to him because of its intrinsic character and range, irrespective of its fame as the region where the bouncing bomb of World War II Dambusters fame was once tested, or its attraction to a generation of smugglers who were able to locate where their illegal loot had been hidden according to the pebble sizes. It's remarkable, he thinks, just how canny criminals can be, an example perhaps of the triumph of necessity over desperation, or, maybe more likely, the smugglers were just bloody clever. He spends more than an hour walking briskly along this natural jewel of nature before eventually returning to the central area of Weymouth town, taking in as he does so the multi-coloured and highly attractive harbour with its seemingly endless rows of private boats, all of which he rather envies, even the smaller fishing vessels, as well as the rather noisy but completely benign groups of beer and coffee drinkers who sit en masse outside cafes and pubs in the open air while thoroughly enjoying themselves shooting the breeze on just about every subject under the sun. This is true social activity, no doubt about it, and part of his solitary self wants a piece of it before it's too late. That's yet another contradiction in his character, or perhaps it's more a question of always wanting something that someone else has but you don't. He sighs remorsefully but quietly, and then swings round to the town's esplanade and takes in for the umpteenth time the striking grandeur of the statue of King George III in the public town square. By this point, it is almost lunchtime and so he returns to what he sees as his private castle where he can continue with his life's routine. It's certainly possible to be boring and interesting at the same time. Nothing in this life is ever simple, and he is no exception.

He has a naturally impatient nature and is unable to wait until the evening to look at the second film reel though he can't help but feel a mild *frisson* of anxiety when he thinks of what it might show. He has already received one warning though that had been a rather gentle, though somewhat ominous, one in the form of a dream. Despite his nascent concern, at exactly two-thirty in the afternoon he slides the DVD into the machine and fast forwards to the second reel of the home movie. Nothing is going to escape his gaze this time.

After the momentary white and yellow flashes, their jagged edges obscuring the entire screen while almost appearing to merge into each other, a clearer set of images slowly materialises before him. This time, the film records a beach holiday his family took in 1964 in the rather chic tourist resort of Juan-les Pins on the French Côte d'Azur, next door to the fashionable town of Antibes. He would have been ten years old, so it was shot just two years after the previous reel. Slowly coming into jerky focus, Roger has vague, and perhaps subliminal, recollections of that period in his young life. The camera first focuses on his furiously waving and laughing mother, who is seen stretched out lazily on a green deckchair on the fine sandy beach, still continuing to be a little on the plump side and yet showing the rather fine bone structure that would serve her so well in her more mature years when for certain reasons she became considerably thinner. He has a transient glimpse of his father, a short stocky man, mildly overweight and with jet black hair swept back over his head in typical 1960's style and a self-confident but still friendly smile as he says something amusing to his wife which the camera does not record as it transmits no sound.

This was fifty years ago, after all, before the arrival of our modern inventions and advanced technology. There follows a rather impressive attempt at a sweeping panoramic view of the beach and coastline, and also the welcoming blue grandeur of the Mediterranean Sea which had an enticing and delicious warmth to it that he can still recall with some pleasure. These pictures must have been taken by his older brother, he reasons, as Peter is nowhere to be seen and why else would the film show both his parents? He himself would not have been able to control the relatively heavy and large cine camera at that age, and, besides, the film also shows a rather intimate image of his younger self who appears to be in a serious conversation with his doomed older sister Margaret.

He is struck by the intelligent look young Roger seems to maintain throughout though he does break off from time to time to stare intensely at the camera and wave his hands around to create some kind of effect. What exactly that was meant to signify he has no idea at all, but he puts it down to the combined immaturity and disinhibition of children. He thinks he is skinnier than he might have imagined and also remembers that around this time, just before he took his eleven-plus qualifying examinations, he had some kind of problem with swallowing and getting food inside him so shortly before this there would have been considerable and sudden weight loss. He can't remember, however, exactly how that problem was resolved. Perhaps it just went away by itself like so many real or supposed childhood ailments. He can even see his ribs sticking out, though clearly he must have avoided too much sun exposure since his bare skin was still so pale. That was fortunate for his adult self. While the rest of his family eventually suffered from different types of skin cancer, he was luckier and did not.

The camera then focuses for about a minute – a surprisingly long time – on Margaret. At that time, she would have been twelve years old and would be killed by a lorry two years later though of course neither she nor anyone else had any inkling or premonition whatsoever of that disaster. What truly strikes Roger is the look the girl gives to the camera as it is an almost identical one to that given by his younger self in the previous reel. Margaret is clearly a very pretty young girl and he can only imagine just how beautiful an older woman she might have eventually become. She inclines her head slightly to the right (his left of course) and gives what can only be described as a girlish but also coquettish smile which seems to be out of sync with her age and experience. Then she gives the intense stare which so unnerves him as if she is also trying to tell him something, or even warn him. This makes no sense to him and he views the rest of the reel with little emotion, an absence that is made easier by the relative mundanity of what he sees. The rest is just a boring home movie, or at least tedious to anyone not actually in it. At the end of that second film reel he turns off the machine, sits down in his favourite armchair and starts to think and reminisce. The two are not the same.

Later that afternoon, he does what he knows is unwise and thinks about loss. In particular, he recalls the happy childhood memories with Margaret when she was already a precocious young woman right up until her sudden and violent death on the roads when she was just fourteen. The enduring memory is one of her kindness to him and the affectionate way in which she would always comfort him when he was upset, which, so far as he can remember, was most of the time. Roger was quite a troubled little boy who enjoyed a few physical pleasures in life, such as swimming in the warm sea and eating ice cream with chocolate topping, but spent most of the time with a long face and a permanently morose persona. He had obviously brightened up a lot since then but he still had this unfortunate tendency to experience extreme melancholia, and whatever people might say about him, there really was little he could ever do about it. It was just his essential nature, the product no doubt of the mixing up of his genes and a personality that had a distinct similarity to his beloved paternal grandfather Ben who also tended to live in a permanent state of misery and misanthropy

When he thinks of the death of his wife Caroline, who also had this unusual ability to comfort him with great tenderness whenever he became distressed or had some major disappointment, which was more often than he might have hoped when a younger man, he feels a sharp sense of unfairness. Why had the two people whom he had truly loved more than any other been taken away from him so cruelly? And why do some favoured folk have all the luck in the world and yet some people like him have to suffer so much? The answer of course, which somehow eluded him, is that life is just life and is always random like a lottery. As is the case with 'mother nature', life is neither fair nor unfair, neither cruel nor kind. Life does not care about him or anyone else in particular. When we attach emotional labels to its results, these merely reflect our own human nature and the erroneous perception of our central importance in the world. Nevertheless, no one can help feeling sadness and joy at what life throws at us and Roger is no exception. So he sits motionless in his armchair on a sunny May afternoon and remembers. As he does so, his eyes first well up with tears and then the salty drops run down from his eyes to his cheeks. He does not actively sob but the deep sadness is there all the same.

That night, he didn't expect to dream about the film he'd seen during the previous day. But unfortunately he did. There was nothing he could do to prevent it, but he wasn't really surprised when it happened. These days there is very little that can surprise him. But the problem is what happens during the nights when he is asleep. Then he has no control.

He drifted effortlessly to sleep within a few minutes of laying his head down. When he woke up at two-thirty in the morning with his pyjamas drenched in sweat, despite the night being cool, he was able to recall all the details of the dream with the same precision as the previous night. The first part seemed pleasant and innocuous enough, with the trademark jerkiness of the handheld cine camera and the pleasant seaside vistas unfolding slowly in sequence. His father was not to be seen at all, but the photographer captured his scrawny self, this time his older brother Peter who is so tall that he towers above his two siblings, and finally a close-up view of his sister Margaret. He feels an intense desire to hold her tight and an even greater desire to speak to her. So he does. It is a dream after all, even if it's a rather dangerous one. As before, he had an eerie awareness that everything surrounding him was not real but just a dream, but he had no desire to wake up from it either naturally or deliberately.

'Do you recognise me Margaret?' Roger asks her in a soft voice (which is usual for him).

'Of course,' the girl replies. 'You're Roger, and all grown up aren't you?'

'Yes, I can't have changed that much then.'

'No,' says Margaret, who starts to stare at him intensely.

Roger begins to feel uneasy, and also dizzy, but continues.

'So I don't scare you then? You know I'm not some kind of dangerous stranger.'

'Of course you're not. You're my brother Roger of course. I always said you would be a handsome man. And you are, though that hasn't really helped you much has it?'

He was confused rather than flattered when he heard this, it felt a bit inappropriate he thought. 'Thank you for the compliment. I didn't expect it. But what about you? You seem so concerned.'

Margaret stares at him again, more directly this time and without blinking even once. 'No Roger, it is you who should be concerned.'

'Me?' he replies. 'Why should I be concerned?'

'You need to be careful. You don't want to be part of my history do you?'

He didn't quite know how to take this or how to answer but it was certainly scary.

Margaret removed a wine gum from her small pink purse and placed it gently into her mouth. 'Roger, I won't say this again. You need to be careful. Take care.'

At that point, she smiled briefly, but without moving her eyes which he found quite disconcerting, then turned around sharply and walked away from him and the others towards the water's edge where she stopped and just stood still without the slightest movement.

Then he woke up.

Though he did have two more dreams during that night, the final one occurring just before he woke up for a second time, they were of little consequence and lacked the clear and dramatic import of that first dream of the night. But he still had no idea at all whether what he had dreamt had any corporeal significance.

IV

The following morning he did not feel in the least bit refreshed, as he should have been after a good night's rest, but tired and agitated to the extent that he was beginning to lose his normally firm hold on what is real in the world and what is not. He has always been aware of his intrinsic tendency to depression, so far never a very serious one despite the two tragedies in his own life, but he has been destabilised before by the unpredictable vagaries of life and he has an uncomfortable feeling that the cosy little world he's so carefully constructed for himself is in real danger of implosion. To misquote Oscar Wilde, one warning dream may have been an accident but to have a second, almost identical, in the same medium is more akin to carelessness. As always with these matters, the key thing is to decide whether it is a problem in his consciousness or a much more profound disruption of space and time. He has a broad mind, and has never believed in the supernatural or ghosts, but at the same time he has always had respect for the evidence that is perceived by his own senses. 'Seeing is believing' may seem a rather trite mantra, but it also has a ring of truth to it, assuming, of course, that one has not been deliberately tricked either by another person's deceit or by a misinterpretation of a phenomenon of nature.

With these confusing and conflicting thoughts whirling uncontrollably in his so-called rational mind, Roger sprang out of bed and started his essential though, to many observers, boring and strictly time-regimented daily regime: washing, dressing, twenty minutes against maximum resistance on his ancient but reliable exercise bicycle during which he listens to classical music punctuated by infuriatingly banal adverts, the same breakfast which never varies even slightly, skim-reading the daily broadsheet newspaper's depressingly familiar obituaries which he scrutinises ever-more closely, more teeth cleaning and then finally his one-hour morning walk to the esplanade, seafront and town centre. The reality is that for a lonely person, even one still grieving for a lost partner, without the existence of a formal structure to the day, life could easily crumble into a form of personal anarchy. He may fritter away much of his time, but at least he is able to do this through his own choice, and he is able to waste his time in a controlled manner. If there is any contradiction in terms to any of this, then he is unaware of it. He should be.

But he also sees a strangely positive side to the dream he has just experienced, even though it may be seen by some as rather perverse. At this stage of his life, he is increasingly unconcerned by what other people think of him, though he is always an unusually polite person in everyday discourse. He thinks he gets that characteristic from his early schooling and his father. Whether or not it was real or imagined – and he knows full well that it could not possibly be real – he had a kind of reunion with his dead sister, for whom his love had become even stronger as an adult than it had been during the first few years after she'd died so suddenly and violently under the wheels of a massive lorry. He vaguely remembers during his early adolescent years that there was a protracted and acrimonious legal case and the lorry driver had lost his job but had not been jailed. Even if he'd been put inside for dangerous or reckless driving it would have solved absolutely nothing. His heartbroken parents were too mired in their awful grief to think too much about a sense of revenge. That's what real grief does to a person. Their marriage was never quite the same after Margaret's death as it seemed that their combined adoration of their beautiful and sweet-natured daughter had provided some form of glue that kept their relationship together and alive. When the source of that binding material had been so suddenly taken away from them, he felt that their marriage, never a particularly close or successful one, had deteriorated in every aspect, though they did, it must be said, stay together to the bitter end of both their lives. That was not a good example of the longstanding Institution of marriage. He had been much luckier, at least for a while.

Roger knew what was coming next in the home movie, and at least he realised that this time he was likely to be amused as well as disturbed. It was a short record of his bar mitzvah which is meant to mark the official transition from childhood into Jewish manhood. He thinks that is pretty nonsensical as no adolescent is a man at thirteen years of age, but his parents, neither of whom was particularly religious, felt obliged to subject him to this ritual, one which he remembers as more of an ordeal than a pleasure. He rather thinks they did it more for their own self-respect than for their son's spiritual and emotional development. Be that as it may, it was a record of a real event after all and he knew that the vast majority of the people in the film would be dead by now. But that only added to the anticipated mystique. Though he was brought up in the Jewish faith, both his parents being Jewish, and members of a liberal congregation in a London synagogue, he lost all faith in any religion after he was thirteen since when he had become an avowed agnostic. Until that time he had been an assiduous scholar of the Old Testament and was a regular attender at the local Hebrew class, a language he had mastered very quickly as he was a bright lad. His immediate and extended family had all changed their original Polish name of Kaminski to Cosgrove around 1937, both because of a real or imagined concern about anti-Semitism and, in the case of those serving in the armed forces during the Second World War, a morbid fear of being captured by the Germans and then handed over to the Nazis and their Gestapo torturers and murderers. While a few of his relatives, most now deceased, opted to revert to their original Polish name when the war was over, most of them, including his own immediate family, retained the anglicised surname of their forbears. During the war, several members of his extended family, mainly great uncles and aunts and their close relatives who were living in various European cities, were ferreted out by the Nazis and taken to various concentration camps, some going to the infamous Auschwitz, where they were all gassed to death apart from just two who, miraculously, had survived the death camps through a combination of luck, guile and personal strength with an intense desire to survive. As a boy, he remembers meeting these two survivors who had a rather strange, almost conspiratorial, appearance; their oddly haunted demeanour created a strong and lasting impression on his teenage self. Some of these terrible fates had been unearthed by Roger's relatives from the detailed records of Yad Vashem in Jerusalem. Perhaps because of his English name and non-Semitic features, he had never personally been the brunt of ignorant anti-Semitic comments but he still derived a rather morbid pleasure when he could shock an offending anti-Semite with the well-placed revelation that he himself was a member of the tribe, one which he would point out had so far produced over two hundred Nobel Prize winners including a certain physicist called Albert Einstein.

He was unable to wait very long after eating his usual light lunch, almost masochistic in its frugality, and immediately afterwards he inserted the DVD into the player and fast forwarded to the third reel. For some reason he felt uncomfortable about leaving the disc in the machine overnight so he had removed it on every occasion after he'd viewed it. Whenever he re-inserted it into the machine, the first reel was always the one that appeared so he had to wind it forwards. After the now familiar transient whiteout and flash he saw a vaguely familiar group of men and women, mostly around forty-five years old he would estimate, all talking to each other in a curiously dated and convivial manner, and dressed formally for the occasion, long elegant evening dresses in the case of the women and black bow ties and formal dinner jackets for the men, some of whom were smoking cigarettes or cigars. His first thought was that the collective joviality just about everyone displayed had a false ring to it, and most of the guests certainly looked rather self-conscious before the prying lens of the camera. The second was that little had probably changed since then though he was sure that for various cogent reasons people didn't go to each other's houses for large dinner parties or other receptions like they used to.

Boxed DVD sets, multiple TV channels, better and more accessible restaurants and changes in people's social behaviour probably accounted for some of that difference, but he still thought back to those halcyon days with more than a little nostalgia. What he can never be sure about when experiencing that regretful feeling is whether his tastes were just different many years before, making him remember falsely, or whether social interaction and fine food really had deteriorated since what he now thinks of as the golden years of his life. But everything becomes blurred and more benign in retrospect. Even the most reviled politician or leader can be remembered with a degree of warmth and nostalgia when viewed in historical terms. The exception to that is grief which may become a little blunted with the passage of time but can also prevent one from ever living life to the full again. Is that what has happened to him?

The images are less jerky and the general appearance of the film is far smoother than the other reels which, Roger soon reasons, is due to the work of a semi-professional camera operator, whom he even now remembers as being a short, rather obese, prematurely bald and very friendly friend of his father, and a man who had shown him particular kindness, and had surreptitiously stuffed three pounds notes (a lot of money in those days) into his jacket pocket, an act of touching generosity that was both unexpected and totally unnecessary.

He is amazed at just how young he looks and, even if he says so himself, he appears to be a rather good-looking boy with remarkably clear, fresh features and luxurious brown hair. He sees a line of people, first his father, then his mother and then himself, all turned out immaculately and serially shaking the hands of one guest after another, a few of whom either openly or quietly give him small envelopes of cash which he would later hand to his father, a still painful process that probably contributed to his lifelong fiscal integrity. Everyone has at least some good points whatever the rest of the world might think of them. Every now and then, a woman kisses him on the cheek, something that he is clearly not enjoying, and once or twice he actually rubs the planted lipstick off his face in disgust with his silk handkerchief. His mother would by then have been about forty-two years old and was beginning to emerge from a post-war trademark dowdiness into a distinctly attractive woman with long brown hair, clear facial features and generous but stylish proportions, an unusual reversal of the usual transition from youth to early middle age. His father, however, seems unchanged, and has a certain self-confident swagger that belies what he always suspected had been quietly lurking beneath the amusing outgoing exterior. He wears large brown-framed glasses, his black hair, now greying at the edges, is swept back as usual and one can sense his powerful frame that for now was held in check by his standard dinner suit that was probably just a little too tight for him. Beware the man who always tries to be so funny. Such people are often the most miserable people on the planet.

The next few frames show Roger and his mother dancing a slow waltz on the enormous ballroom floor, something they had practised endlessly at home the day before until they had the coordinated steps down to a fine art. They are about the same height, an equality that was to change over the ensuing years of his growth spurt as in adulthood he stood a good eight inches taller than she. That is not actually saying a lot as she was only five feet tall at most. Brief glimpses appear for seconds on the landscape of the film record of his much taller older brother, who would have been seventeen at the time, as well as all four of his grandparents. He only remembers one of them with any degree of warmth and that was his paternal grandfather to whom he would remain close for decades until his death at the fine age of ninety-nine years. Now that was a good innings for sure. The other three he even now regards as unremarkable people. He just about recognises the odd aunt and uncle and various second cousins and even more distant relatives, some of whom he had never even met or heard of, whose images traverse the screen for a few seconds only.

The final picture shows his young self in more serious mode as he uses a long knife to cut up a huge square-shaped white cake with gold lettering saying *'With love from Roger on his special occasion'* shown clearly on its top half. He manages to divide the cake with commendable precision and then pretends to lick the knife, thereby providing convincing evidence of his intrinsic immaturity despite what was clearly a fine emerging intelligence. But of course his adored sister Margaret is nowhere to be seen as she had died the year before. No wonder he perceives a subtle air of sadness in the faces of all the people he sees, as they would doubtless all have been more than aware of the tragedy that had befallen his family. But everyone he sees certainly puts on a good show of joy. Was that British stiff upper lip, or an overwhelming desire to forget the past and enjoy the occasion, or just the effects of alcohol and the moment?

As he stepped out of his day clothes and slowly donned his pyjamas, Roger had little doubt that he would have a disturbing dream about the bar mitzvah reception that he'd viewed on the cine film earlier that day. Indeed he even tried to be mentally prepared for it and began to work out in his mind the possible forms such a dream might take, assuming of course that it really is a dream that he has to experience during the night and not another nightmare. He is not completely certain about the difference between the two as it's really a matter of degree and a subjective assessment. But in reality, you just know if you've had a nightmare. You don't have to think about it. Besides, they are usually much easier to recall than the pleasant dreams.

He was neither mistaken nor disappointed, though the form it took did surprise him somewhat. He fell asleep very quickly – within a few minutes – and woke up sweating and fearful again about three hours later in the middle of the night. His dream took him very quickly right inside the reception hall which appeared exactly like the recorded image taken fifty years before. He found himself as well dressed as the guests, something that was most unusual for him since he never wears a 'black tie' suit whatever the occasion. The most formal attire for him is invariably the humble lounge suit. He smiled benignly at the various men, women, adolescents and children all of whom seemed to smile back at him but at the same time they appeared to look straight through him which he found eerie and strangely disconcerting, even for a dream. But again, he knew exactly what state he was in. That in itself is not a normal characteristic of most dreams and should have alerted him even though in a sense that was of course just not possible except in retrospect when recalling the experience afterwards when he awoke. Finally he spots his younger self sitting alone on a chair with his elbows resting on a large round table on which the remains of a delicious finger buffet were scattered. The boy Roger looks up at him and gives him the same intense and all- knowing stare as before.

'All the smoked salmon bridge rolls have been taken,' he complains to Roger.

He smiles and decides to engage with the boy who is certainly better looking than he had always been given to understand by his parents.

'I'm so sorry about that. I guess there are a lot of hungry people around.'

'Pigs you mean. All they think of is how much they can shove into their mouths. How come all the smoked salmon rolls go first?'

He has some sympathy with this view which he vaguely remembers. 'Because I imagine they taste the best.'

Then they look at each other for about ten seconds during which neither of them says a word. The boy, or more accurately the newly emerged man, breaks the silence.

'I'm sorry, I don't want to be rude or anything, but don't I know you from somewhere?' Roger is not quite sure how to respond to this but speaks with caution.

'You probably do. I'm actually a friend of the family…'

'You mean my parents?'

'Well yes, something like that,' he replies.

'I see,' the boy says but not without a distinctly sceptical look in his intelligent eyes.

Roger goes on warily.

'We've all known each other for a long time you see.'

The boy seems not quite convinced.

'Were you and my Dad at school together by any chance?'

'Funnily enough, we weren't and anyway I'm a lot older than he is.'

'Well you don't really look it. My dad looks much older than he is and maybe you look much younger than you are. That's why I thought you might know him.'

'I shall take that as a compliment.'

The boy smiles at this.

'Well you can take it any way you want but there is, if you don't mind me saying so, something very familiar about you that I just can't work out.'

Roger is intrigued by the boy's insight. But he becomes less impressed when he realises he is talking to himself when he was much younger. It just isn't right to be complimenting yourself. 'You are remarkably insightful for your age if I may say so.'

'You may. Other people have said the same thing to me, but it doesn't help me at school. Some of the other pupils in my class like me and others hate me. They say I'm arrogant and selfish.'

'That just isn't true,' Roger reassures him. 'They're probably just jealous of your maturity and brain power.'

'Oh I wish that were true but, you know, I don't think so. Some of them just hate my guts. Hey, maybe they're anti-Semitic.'

'But with a name like Cosgrove how would they know?'

The boy smiles knowingly at this.

'They bloody well know alright. They always find out these things and they know I'm not a Christian. Also my father – he certainly looks Jewish don't you think?'

'I couldn't say,' he lied.

After this friendly exchange the boy stares at him again and then speaks quietly.

'It's funny because I don't even know your name but you're the kind of person I really hope I grow up to be like. You are kind, wise and don't judge people. You take them as they are. But there's just one thing I want to say to you. Please be careful. You must be careful.'

V

As Roger was making his first cappuccino of the morning after what was again a decidedly disturbing night's sleep, he tried to make some kind of sense out of what he'd experienced over these last three days. In simple terms, all that had happened is that he'd had some very vivid dreams that were clearly based on and catalysed by what he had seen in an old home movie the previous day. There was no mystery to that and probably nothing to be unduly worried about. But on the other hand, in all three cases he had had some extremely vivid experiences in which he felt entirely involved with and connected to all the people in the dreams, and in every case either his younger self or his dead sister had warned him to be careful. But be careful of what? He was already sixty-three years old, albeit a youthful and well-preserved man, so this could not have meant sudden death at a young age. But maybe he was being warned of a looming danger in the present time, perhaps even in the following week. Or perhaps the children in the dream had no idea of his subsequent life and relative success so they saw things only from their own limited temporal view.

The more he thought about these questions, the more confused and uncertain he became, and the more absurd the whole notion began to seem. He also wondered whether he was more mentally disturbed than he'd initially thought by just about everything bad that had happened in his life. Yet he was still privileged in so many ways – he was healthy, well educated, relatively well-off financially with a generous University pension, and living in a picturesque cottage in a particularly beautiful part of the country. It was also true that he had two fine sons and was on friendly terms with his older brother, not to mention his few close friends, but he knew he was still grieving for Caroline and was more than aware of his intense loneliness. To an extent, that was his own choice at this vulnerable time, but he couldn't go on like this forever. Was everything he was experiencing during these days and nights just the result of his accumulated unhappiness and distress? Were the dreams merely his brain's method of dealing with life's traumas and disappointments? Not knowing the answers to these questions only added to his anxiety and distress. But he must keep going at all costs. If only he knew the answers. But he didn't. He will understand, but not yet.

He's not quite sure what the fourth reel of the movie will have in store for him, though he has a rough idea of its contents from his rapid run through when he first skimmed all five reels. While he is aware of the time period, he doesn't know what effects the visions will have on his already battered psyche. He recalls he was fifteen at the time which would put the date at the end of the summer of 1969, a year when he can vaguely remember the Beatles still playing together as a group, or at least just about, and he was studying hard for his trial Ordinary level examinations scheduled for the following autumn. At least he doesn't need to retake those, though he did have a disturbing dream quite recently in which he did, and that really frightened him. He certainly wouldn't pass them now. He knows their holiday that year was spent mainly in an alpine town in the Swiss Alps, and that there were only three of them – his two parents and himself as his older brother was already far too old for a family vacation.

After going through what had now become an almost immutable exercise regime, walking briskly outside while taking in the satisfying elegance of the pretty town and the grandeur of the pure blue skyscape gently framing the seashore, Roger wolfed his usual meagre lunch and made his way into the cottage's one and only living room. There he made himself comfortable in his favourite armchair, inserted the DVD into the player and wound the film forward until a picture duly appeared announcing the arrival of holiday reel four. This time there is only the briefest white and red flash before he sees a grainy picture of the family car, a Ford Zephyr this time, slowly and painfully descending backwards down the shared driveway of their London home. He wonders just what was inside their suitcases to make the car strain so much, and he suspects it was the many tins of food and soup, a necessary precaution for a household that was still no stranger to relative austerity.

His mother always ensured that her family was well fed. Indeed, when the picture quickly changes without warning to the front of their expensive Swiss hotel, Roger is struck by how much his younger self has 'filled out' which he always knew was the euphemism of the day for saying he was on the plump side. That was certainly true, although he wasn't actually fat, and his mother had somehow kept the family balance in a sense since she appeared thinner than before as if two years of worry had literally removed the excess weight from her. The combined weight status of mother and second son managed to perpetuate the status quo. He had never really thought of how she may have suffered at that time. But actually, she did. So did his father, though he had always been aware of that somehow, maybe because it was just more obvious. Children are far more observant and insightful than they are generally given credit for. He had learned that lesson many years before.

The next frame showed a clearly terrified fifteen-year-old Roger holding onto the hand of his mother as the whole family slowly ascended the steep face of Mount Jacobshorn in the relative comfort of a cable car. Despite the impressive views from the car, that fear of heights proved to be a permanent fixture of his character. He remembers his terror that the car might suddenly stop and get stranded between staging posts. When they had reached the top of the mountain, which was a large one at about 8500 feet above sea level, they appeared to be more relaxed. His father had captured the moment when his wife and son cautiously emerged from the cable station and carefully walked along a short pathway to a high viewpoint with spectacular views of the surrounding mountains and sky. The camera was then trained downwards to encompass the town of Davos where they were staying in an unusually posh and pricey hotel. Well, his father used to say, you only live once and you can't take it with you. Though there were also fine views of the various ski slopes, this was of little interest to any of them since no one in the family had ever had an interest in skiing. Since 1971, Davos had played permanent host to the World Economic Forum and had gained international fame because of this, but at the time of the film reel that was still two years in the future.

There followed seemingly endless visual sweeps of the surrounding vistas which, even on camera, were truly magnificent with the remarkable clarity that can only be obtained when the air between adjacent snow-capped mountain peaks is so clear and free of pollution. No wonder, Roger reckons, so many tubercular patients in the previous century were sent high up into the Swiss mountains and sanatoria to recuperate and regain their health. Clearly his father was more interested in capturing wonderful mountain scenery than he was in capturing the intermittent but genuine fear that almost paralysed his wife and son. Perhaps that was just as well. At least this way they could all enjoy the film when they returned home. The reality is that at a time when they should all have been thoroughly enjoying the trip, they were far more concerned with their own survival and in managing to control their fear of heights and of falling thousands of feet to the green valley and town below, one that from the summit seemed little bigger than a doll's house.

That evening, Roger thought he might be able to influence his inevitable dreaming in advance through an act of pure will. Something inside him was saying that would be a pretty hopeless task because he was dealing with forces far greater than himself and, besides, dreams have an irritating tendency to occur in whatever form they choose irrespective of the wishes of the dreamer. He knew his clever idea was not clever at all but he tried his best all the same. If someone tells you not to think of baked beans, for example, then in practical terms that is an impossible thing to do. Inevitably you will think of baked beans. Similarly, if you make a conscious decision while awake to have an atraumatic and pleasant dream, then you can be pretty sure that will have no influence at all on what's in store for you during the night (or during the day if you are a night worker). He knows all of this full well – he is a scientist after all – but in spite of this he is as irrational as the rest of us when it comes to his own well-being. So one hour before retiring, he listens to the most relaxing music he knows through his earphones and makes a determined attempt to think only of positive experiences he's had during his life. It was a brave attempt to change the future. But of course it was to no avail.

It took him longer to fall asleep as he was so worried about dreaming and what was to come. But after about an hour of this quasi-alert form of subliminal drowsiness he eventually entered the different stages of sleep around midnight. As always, the deepest period of sleeping occurred in the early hours of the morning, and he again woke up drenched with sweat in the middle of the night. While his dream was in a curious way rather more interesting than the others, it was still more akin to a nightmare and his rather sad attempt while awake to pre-empt its contents had failed miserably. But that was inevitable.

It seemed to begin from nowhere as is the case with all out-of-body experiences. He found himself riding a cable car to the summit of Mount Jacobshorn, while an anxious version of his younger self, then fifteen years old, sat nervously on a low wooden bench directly opposite him, clearly terrified and looking straight ahead to avoid experiencing any of the vertiginous views of the sloping valley beneath them. He felt rather sorry for the boy, who had an open, fresh and completely unlined face with occasional teenage spots, thick wavy brown hair and a definitely intelligent look that was clearly discernible despite the enormous fear and distress he was obviously experiencing. Roger finds this interesting since, though he no longer has the morbid fear of heights which he remembers well from childhood, he still gets an unpleasant ache in his feet and calves whenever he looks down at anything from an appreciable height. He supposes some phobias never resolve completely, even with the passage of time and emotional maturity. Neither of them says anything until they reach the summit of the mountain marked by the upper cable car station. At this point the boy is noticeably more relaxed and the two of them walk together along a short, man-made gravel path to a viewpoint from which the full magnificence of the mountain vistas is revealed in all its grandeur. Though they have not been formally introduced to each other, they both seem to know their respective identities, and for some reason which he can't fathom, neither of the boy's parents is within sight though they had both accompanied him. That surely would not be the case in real life. They both admire the view and the sheer magisterial power of the Albula Alps all around them, one of the great natural wonders of Eastern Switzerland. After what seems a protracted interval, they begin a conversation.

'So how are you enjoying your holiday in Davos, Roger?' he asked the boy.

'It's been fine, thank you. No disasters this time, for once,' was the reply.

'Were you expecting any on this trip?

'Not really. But you never know. And there's plenty of time left yet.'

'Quite, but I'm sure you will all be fine,' Roger says in a reassuring tone.

'Have you read any Plato?' the boy suddenly asks, much to Roger's surprise.

'Yes but that was a long time ago. It did make an impression though.'

'How long ago was that?'

'Oh it must have been when I was about fifteen or sixteen.'

Roger then gasps involuntarily as he realises the rather alarming timing behind his words. But the boy either hasn't noticed or else is unfazed.

'Right, the same as me then… I just love *The Symposium*, don't you?'

'As far as I can remember that was one of his best…'

'It is his best and it's also so modern don't you think?'

At this point, Roger decides to bluff.

'Yes I entirely agree. By the way, what other philosophy books have you read?'

'Oh a lot, I'm really into philosophy you know. I also love Hume though I have to admit I'm struggling a bit with Kant.'

'Yes, he is a bit obscure isn't he?' he replies.

'Absolutely,' the boy says, 'but Kant is so very penetrating, isn't he?'

'For sure he is that, though in my opinion, many of the great philosophers have been extremely clear and lucid and not opaque.' Roger does actually believe this.

'Yes I suppose you're right.'

'Tell me Roger, do you know what you will do when you are fully grown up?' The boy is silent for a few seconds while he appears to think carefully.

'I'm not entirely sure. I'll probably do science in the sixth form after the O-levels are out of the way, and I may need to study biology to keep all my options open. Anyway, that's what my dad keeps telling me. You must always keep your options open.'

'Well, if I may say so, that's very good advice. But tell me something, have you ever considered studying medicine at University? It gives you a lot of options.'

'No I don't want to be a doctor. It's not my thing.'

'Well you must do what most interests you.'

After this brief but friendly exchange, the atmosphere between them becomes noticeably more strained as the focus of their conversation suddenly changes.

The boy speaks first.

'Sorry, I don't mean to be rude at all, but I'm sure we've met before.'

'No, I don't think so,' Roger replies.

The boy is unconvinced.

'Well, I think we have. You seem very familiar to me, but I can't quite put my finger on it.'

'I think it must be a case of mistaken identity.'

'Well maybe you're right… But, and please don't take this the wrong way, from our brief talk I am really impressed with how you treat me as a real person and don't talk down to me like most of my teachers at school. I can't stand some of them. They really irritate me.'

Roger can't help feeling just a little flattered at this compliment from a clearly very intelligent and sensitive young man.

'Thank you. I'm glad you think that.'

The boy then adopts a mock serious expression as a prelude to saying something he thinks is very important.

'But there is just one thing I must say to you, whoever you are.' 'And what's that if I may ask?'

'Be careful. You really must be careful. I have a strong sense that you are in real danger.' 'But in danger from what Roger?'

The boy looks at him again with an intense expression that somehow seems very familiar. 'Just be very careful.'

Then he woke up. It happened as suddenly as he had fallen asleep.

VI

The dreams of the previous four nights had left Roger in no doubt whatsoever that his life was in some kind of danger, though he had no idea what danger was in store for him or even where it might come from or how he could possibly prevent it. In a way, his fears were irrational because these warnings had come to him in dreams and not in the real world. While he fully recognises this, nevertheless he's only human and, critically, he has a completely open mind for almost everything that happens in the world despite his rational way of thinking. But there is no middle ground here. Either the warnings are true, in which case there must be physical laws outside the realm of what is known, or else the whole thing is nonsensical, in which case he's worrying for nothing and the only reality is what he perceives in his everyday life. While logic dictates that the second of these possibilities is by far the most likely, rather to his surprise he finds himself totally in thrall to the first explanation, though he knows that might make him just a little crazy in more than one sense.

Having decided what he believes to be true, the next task is to formulate a plan of action. Yet he doesn't know where the threat to his life is coming from. It could be a random accident on the road, for instance, in which he could be killed, or worse, seriously maimed for life, or perhaps another person, known or unknown to him, is determined to kill or injure him –perhaps some disgruntled former student who wants to get back at him for not being awarded a top examination grade. It could also herald a severe illness, but that is far less likely, not only because he feels fit and well, but also because that would be more akin to a natural, though unfortunate event, and not something that could be avoided. He reasons that if he has been given a warning, then by definition it should be possible to prevent the dangerous thing, whatever it is, happening to him. It was not knowing what to expect that was as disconcerting as the ominous nature of the warning itself. Yet if he is too careful and cautious in his everyday life, that would drastically limit the quality of his existence and make him so absurdly risk-averse that he'd be afraid to venture outside his front door. No, that would be completely unacceptable. Yes, he would be a little more cautions when crossing the road or connecting home appliances to electricity sockets, but he would certainly not make any significant change to his daily routine. Life is boring and painful for him already without the added burden of paranoia. There would be no plan of action. And that was his plan.

But he still had a decision to make. There was one more film reel to view and that was reel number five. This was taken by his father in 1971 when he would have been seventeen years old, and he remembers it as the last time he went on holiday with his parents. He can just about remember some of the details, but most vivid of all was the memory of the almost constant rain. It had been a driving holiday, travelling in their spacious Rover car to the picturesque but frequently wet Lake District region of North-West England with a few further days exploring the West Highlands of Scotland where, as he recalls, it also rained continuously for the four days or so they had spent there, beautiful as the scenery undoubtedly was.

He thinks most of the cine film had been shot during the first week in England and the pictures would only have been of his mother and himself, his older brother being elsewhere of course, doing his own holiday thing. Roger thought about not looking at the film at all and then seeing if he still had a warning dream, rather like a controlled scientific experiment, but on further reflection he felt he should just face whatever nightmares, warnings or other horrors life might have in store for him. He had reached the stage of life when he was more afraid of what he perceived as moral cowardice than confronting the premonition of his own extinction.

Increasingly, he was beginning to see the home movie reels as having a life of their own, with an organic existence that was able somehow to exist independently of being viewed, and with a supernatural ability to connect to people in the living world. The exquisite visions of his family, mainly seen on summer holidays, not only brought back vivid memories of his past, but also had the ability to influence his behaviour in the present time. While that notion would normally have frightened him beyond measure, something within his psyche, already weighed down with an understandable melancholia from his personal tragedies, also perceived it as something positive, an opportunity to explore and to somehow live a better and more fulfilled life. While that perception may sound a little far-fetched, or at least eccentric, it is nevertheless a genuine description of how he felt about the whole business.

With these thoughts and such motivation uppermost in his mind, Roger prepared himself mentally for a confrontation with the final reel of the movie. This he decided to do just after his usual frugal lunch, though he thought it best to drink two cups of strong coffee in order to be better prepared for what was to come. He needed all the help he could get. As before, he saw each episode as having two phases. The first was merely observation during which he presumed the movie images were burned into his subconscious. But then came the second phase in which his mind did not control events because the events clearly controlled him.

As he had done on all the previous occasions, he carefully inserted the DVD into the player and fast forwarded the film until he reached the fifth reel. He had already managed a brief glimpse of its contents nearly a week before, and he wasn't startled by the fleeting white and yellow flash, its edges strangely jagged rather like a transient explosion of colour. Almost immediately, he saw a familiar scene of what he knew to be the mighty, yet also rather gentle, grey mountains of the Lake District, one of his favourite beauty spots in England which he's visited with Caroline many times. Though the rugged and seemingly contiguous mountain peaks were elegant sheets of grey stone, the middle and lower grass-covered slopes leading up to them were like green velvet, and in the distance he recognised the town of Keswick abutting the strikingly picturesque Derwent Water where they had often stayed in the early days of their marriage. But this vision was a memory of a time many years before that, and he would not have been able even now to tell the difference between the sight before him and the present, even though this represented an interval approaching fifty years. Such elegant and natural beauty is timeless and is seemingly immune to the ageing process which, if it occurs at all, only adds to the gentle harmony that exists between the mountains, the lakes and the land in between.

The handheld cine camera producing the jerky images switches its attention to a rather sad event in which a seventeen-year-old Roger is posing rather self-consciously with his mother while they both try to shield themselves from a particularly heavy downpour with what are clearly small and inadequate umbrellas. They both look utterly miserable in the rain, especially his mother who wears a light-blue raincoat and a tired expression, while Roger appears rather more accepting of the weather which is nevertheless dull, grey and wet. There are cogent geographical and climatological reasons why this sublime region suffers from so much rainfall, but remarkably it does not necessarily detract from its unquestionable natural beauty. But clearly his mother is less than impressed and he recalls that she always did enjoy sunbathing in the Italian and French Riviera far more than rain-soaked holidays in Britain. While the tranquil views of the surrounding green mountains, Borrowdale Valley, Keswick and Derwent Water that can be seen from the ascending slopes and summit of the gentle Latrigg Fell manage to energise Roger with inspiration and admiration, by contrast, in his mother's case, these sights fall on eyes that can see but are unable to appreciate. Or to put it more crudely, the eyes look but do not see. Ah well, *chacun à son goût* as the French say. There follows a rather repetitive sequence of mountain images with one long-range shot of Roger rapidly ascending another fell, with all the efficiency of a mountain goat. Despite his underlying fear of heights, it was invariably trumped by an even more powerful love of a surfeit of natural beauty.

He let the film run until the very end of the DVD, the final image being of a white sheet rapidly merging into a reddish edge effect and then to a final state of oblivion in which there was nothing to see whatsoever, the proverbial end of the road so to speak. Roger was certainly impressed by the stunning scenery captured so clearly by his father, but was also rather sad to see the look of misery on his mother's face as opposed to the one of discomfort alone on his former self's face. He wondered, not without some sense of moderate trepidation it must be said, what dreams such a visual experience would engender that night. He would not have very long to find out, and his sense of curiosity also hoped he would finally get some credible answers to his uncertainty about the future. But he didn't really think he would, no matter how prepared he might be to face any danger.

He was increasingly restless during the rest of the day, in part because he was full of anticipation for what was to come that night – he had a rather irrational conviction that he was about to find out the answer to his uncertainty and the riddles and warnings he'd received. He thought it unlikely that nothing would be resolved, but he would need to be eternally vigilant during his entire life for an ever-present danger. Reality, even when it is a false reality that occurs in a dream or a nightmare, seldom measures up to one's expectations. Why do we all make that mistake?

Within ten minutes of laying his head down on the soft pillow, he fell fast asleep. He'd gone to bed late that night, or at least late for him, at eleven-thirty to help sleep and experience the inevitable dream. When he awoke from a deep sleep three hours later he was rather confused, but for once he wasn't sweating, though that might have something to do with the deliberate absence of blankets: it was, after all, a particularly warm night that May. In the dream, which seemed in retrospect to be very short (which, like the others, it probably was in real time), he had found himself scrambling up the steep grassy slopes of Mount Skiddaw, the third-highest peak in England and a continuation of the smaller Lakeland fell of Latrigg that he knew so well. The vistas all around him were as magnificent as in the film reel he had seen during the day, and accompanying him on his right side was his seventeen-year-old self. Though he was increasingly breathless as the climb became steeper, his young companion seemed scarcely out of breath at all even though he was walking as quickly, if not more quickly, than Roger himself. The surreal nature of this juxtaposition strongly suggested to him that he was in the midst of a dream and that it just wasn't real. But that realisation did not make him try to exit the dream by blinking several times (an old trick he always used to employ when he was a child) because even in this unreal state he wanted to get answers if he possibly could. They continue climbing for about three minutes before the youth turns toward him, smiles pleasantly and starts a conversation.

'It really is very good of you to accompany me on this trek,' he says to Roger.

'Delighted,' he replies. 'I'm glad to be here and have your company.'

'I reckon we're almost halfway to the top, but it's not too bad is it?'

'No, it isn't. It's much easier than I thought it would be,' Roger lies, breathlessly.

'Well,' the youth continues, 'it certainly beats studying for A-levels.'

'Absolutely. You have my sympathies there. When

are you taking them?'

'Next summer, but I have the trial exams, or "mocks" in a few months' time…'

'You mean natural sciences – physics, maths and chemistry I presume?' Roger asks.

'Yes, exactly right. You're well informed, but I guess I shouldn't be surprised at that should I?'

'Why do you say that?'

The youth looks at Roger directly and intensely and gives a charming and knowing smile before speaking.

'I think we both know the answer to that, don't you?'

'You mean you already know who I am?' asks Roger, genuinely surprised.

'Of course I do. You must know that I'm unusually bright and precocious for my age.'

'Then who am I?' asks Roger.

His younger self gives him a look of surprised incredulity, and shakes his head slowly. 'Well you're me of course, only in the future when I'm fully grown up and an adult.'

'You're right as I would expect, but you shouldn't equate the two as I know some adults who have never grown up, and that includes some pretty famous people.'

'Good point, but anyway it's still a real pleasure for me to meet you in this way. I won't say I'm honoured because that would somehow be too much like self-congratulation.'

'Yes, I see what you mean about that. It's all pretty subtle stuff isn't it?'

'If you say so,' the youth replies, 'but is there anything in particular that you want to ask me? I promise I will give you my best answer if I possibly can.'

'Well now you mention it…'

'I am mentioning it.'

'I can see that. So here is my question…'

'You mean here is your problem?'

Roger is struck by the youth's tone and relative subtlety.

'Let's just say it's both my question and my problem.'

'So what you are concerned about is both the problem and the point.'

Roger thinks about this for a few seconds before replying.

'Yes that's true in a way…'

'In what way do you mean?'

'In the way I am about to tell you.'

'Right, good sir, so please fire away.'

Roger seems to have a little trouble organising his thoughts, but since he knows the entire scenario is just a dream, a product of his own brain, that is probably not too surprising. But in theory, there is no reason why that realisation should stop him getting answers. Also, the youth seems far too mature in his speech for one so young. It doesn't add up.

'Every time I look at a home movie made by my, I mean our, father and I then dream about it, I get a warning to be careful, but I don't know what I'm meant to be careful of or even when the threat will come.'

The youth looks at Roger in a decidedly serious and mature way and replies slowly. 'Hmm, I see what you mean. That is problematic isn't it?'

'Yes, very problematic.'

'Well I can tell you something, not the whole story you understand, but perhaps enough to make you understand what you need to do.'

'Well,' says Roger, 'that would be a start and more than helpful I'm sure.'

At this point they have reached the mid-point of their slow arduous climb and both of them stop and turn round to look at the mountain peaks and the green valleys that appear to divide them in the distance. Roger feels that they are so near, yet the clear air only creates that illusion as they are mostly many miles away in the distance.

'Magnificent don't you think?' says the youth.

'Absolutely,' Roger agrees, 'that's precisely the best way of describing it.'

At this point, his younger self continues.

'So the important thing is that you will be faced with a very dangerous situation in the not-too-distant future. I know when that will be but I'm afraid I'm not able to tell you exactly when.'

'You mean you can't tell me anything specific?'

'I didn't say that. Look, it's in both our interests for you to be fit and well and to survive the clear danger that could so easily end in tragedy.'

'Well you will know all about that from when your sister Margaret died.'

'Yes, that was a terrible tragedy which caused us all great sadness, and I know you've had another one recently, but that's even more reason for you not to have another one and to be extra careful.'

Roger is stunned that the youth seems to know so much about him.

'But can you give me any idea as to when this danger to me is going to happen? I mean is it tomorrow, or in a few months' time or perhaps many years in the future?'

'You need to be careful in a few years. Until then, all being well and barring unpredictable accidents of course, you should be in no immediate danger.'

'Are you sure there's nothing else you can tell me?'

The youth looks at Roger again and smiles ruefully.

'No Roger, I'm afraid there's not.'

'OK, I'll take care then.'

'Yes, you do that. Good luck and good night.'

VII

DORSET MAY 2040

It had certainly been a busy day for Professor Adrian Cosgrove. Having just about recovered from the visceral shock of his father's sudden death from a massive brain haemorrhage only one week before, and after surviving the painful theatricality of his funeral two days later, he'd spent almost seven hours without a break trying to sort out his possessions. He'd travelled by train from London the previous day to his father's modest but homely cottage in Weymouth, with the express task of dividing up the multitude of items that had been left behind, and trying to instil some kind of order or priority. His older brother Michael and his sister-in-law Susan were due to join him in this daunting endeavour the following day. His father had a vast library of books which seemed to line not only the fitted shelves in his small study and the living room, but also most of the meagre spare space available, whether that was on the floor in the bedroom, behind many of the chairs, beside and below the sideboards or along the kitchen shelves next to the ancient jars of coffee; a few volumes even sequestered under the large double bed. Adrian reckons his father must have had in the region of fifteen hundred books covering a wide variety of subjects, including medicine, science, computing, novels, history, war, and, in fact, probably just about everything. He even had some rather newer books on so-called supernatural events which was certainly a surprise. Clearly he was not the kind of person to just give things away. But, on the other hand, he had no inkling he was going to die suddenly. For that matter, few of us ever do. That's almost certainly a good thing he reckons.

Adrian had always been rather closer to his late father Roger than had his older brother Michael, though both had unquestionably good relations with their parents, particularly their reclusive but thoroughly decent and extremely intelligent father. Adrian, his wife Jacqui and their two lively children had come down from London, usually at least twice per year, for as long as he can remember to visit Roger in his cottage in Weymouth, visits that were a tight fit, if not a little claustrophobic, and which necessitated the hiring of two fold-up beds for the children both of whom adored their generous grandfather. They always equated these short weekend visits with gifts of several bars of the finest dark and milk chocolate, so clearly he knew how to make his adored grandchildren happy. They all especially enjoyed the bracing walks in which he took them along the seafront and town esplanade as well as the longer outings passing beside the bobbing sailing boats in Portland Harbour and then on to the long expanse of Chesil Beach.

The death of his mother Caroline had hit Adrian very hard for sure, but his grief was still no match for the pain it had caused his father who never completely recovered from this major trauma. Roger had never remarried, which was something that worried his few friends but came as no real surprise to his children. He did, however, have a close three-year relationship a decade previously with an attractive and kindly woman called Joan, a vivacious local pharmacist who was a few years younger than he. Sadly, things didn't work out for them long term, and, so far as he is aware, there was never anyone else in his life, but of course no one can see into another's heart however close they might be. There was no question in his children's minds that their nice dad had been a loner for the rest of his life, which amounted to no less than twenty-four years after Caroline's death. That's a long time to grieve for sure. Somehow their father had become stuck in, or even obsessed by, the past.

Fortunately, Roger had the foresight to make a will in which he left his main asset, the cottage, to his two sons, equally divided as they saw fit, as well as a gift to them both of all his financial assets, which were pretty modest it has to be said. There were a few specific bequests to individuals, such as his most prized antiques which he left to some of his friends and academic colleagues (which he did not regard as the same thing), and his horde of eight watches which he left to his four grandchildren, giving two to each of them. He possessed one original and much-loved oil painting of Scafell Pike, the tallest peak in the Lake District, which he left to his old friend Joan as he knew she was particularly fond of it. He had always been a very fair-minded man despite his well-recognised and invariably tolerated eccentricities. But that still left all his books and other bits and pieces to sort out, a task that was far more formidable than either Adrian or Michael had ever considered likely.

But Adrian had a plan. He decided the only way to deal with the mass of his father's possessions and assorted bric-a-brac, which, though largely worthless in monetary terms, was profoundly important in a sentimental way to Roger, was to place everything to be saved in one series of cardboard boxes labelled *'keep'* and to deposit everything else in a separate series of cardboard boxes labelled *'discard'*. But in doing this, he was very aware that he had to make a number of value judgements as to what was deemed worthy and what was not, but anyway he was pretty sure he was making a good job if it. Yet it was still profoundly sad to see and sometimes discard to the rubbish dump what represented the sum total of a long life, one that was, so far as he was able to assess, well lived and at least partially enjoyed.

Talking of living well, Adrian has done pretty well for himself by any standards. He is a Professor of Clinical Immunology at one of the best London teaching hospitals and, at the ripe age of fifty-one (though he could easily pass for a man ten years younger in view of his boyish good looks), he has established an excellent national and international reputation. While working in a famous laboratory in Cambridge University in his late twenties, he made a fundamental discovery about the host response to pathogen invasion, one which actually turned out to be completely true as well as important, and he'd been awarded his chair at a London university at the relatively young age of thirty-six. He was so well regarded by the powers that be that his name was already being discussed for possible nomination to the illustrious Royal Society. But perhaps the most refreshing thing about Adrian is that his real motivation comes entirely from his passion for his subject and not a passion for pure self-advancement. In terms of being a true scientist, he is for certain the proverbial real deal.

As he thinks about his father's life, as well as his own and what it might bring in the future, he finds himself musing almost inevitably on the past. The current year is 2040 so his father would have been sixty-two when his wife Caroline died in 2016, and then he reached the ripe old age of eighty-six before he himself died about a week before. Not a bad innings, he thinks, though by current standards it wasn't a great one either. But then of course, three years after his wife's death, by which time he was well ensconced in his Dorset cottage with a new, and in some ways inferior, kind of life, the coronavirus global pandemic arrived. This had been the cause of the greatest global disruption since the Second World War, and some even think it was worse. Originating from bats in the Wuhan district of China, where it had somehow mysteriously crossed species from bats to humans, the virus had rapidly spread to all corners of the world with the United States, United Kingdom and Brazil being particularly badly affected, especially elderly and vulnerable residents of care homes. Millions of people were infected and there were hundreds of thousands of deaths worldwide until eventually the pandemic ended after about a year of severely, and in some cases permanently, disrupting the entire fabric of society, when an effective vaccine was finally developed to keep most people protected from infection. But the short- and long-term financial and mental health consequences of this unusually cruel virus pandemic were truly devastating with numerous bankruptcies and redundancies, massive post-traumatic stress, increased rates of suicide and widespread economic recessions worldwide.

Adrian was thirty-one years old at that terrible time in 2020, and was working as a final year trainee medical registrar in rheumatology in London where he was a bachelor and living in a small third-floor apartment with no access to a garden. The whole period was profoundly traumatic for him, and also for his older brother Michael, a lawyer, who had just got married and was also living in London. Things were not helped by the mismanagement of the disaster by the government of the day which seemed to do everything wrong, including talking down to people and rarely answering questions directly, yet it also seemed to have political answers, invariably inadequate, to every single criticism. He didn't doubt its good intentions, only its actions, or, to be more specific, its inactions. He can still remember the unprecedented and, in his view, sometimes unjustified restrictions of personal freedoms almost amounting to a 'police state', and then the extraordinarily bitter and ferocious recriminations that followed, near the end of the emergency, aimed at the self-congratulatory government and its 'expert' advisers. These devastating condemnations of the multiple failures to act in the most effective way came from both official reports and from the bereaved relatives of those many thousands of vulnerable people who had died in care homes. He also recalls the repulsive two metre 'social distancing' in which such a culture of fear had been inculcated into people by the government and its scientific advisers that it became virtually impossible to walk along the street without at least a few people looking at you as if you were about to infect them with the bubonic plague. Adrian would never forget the look of sheer terror in people's eyes, while the widespread notion of communal kindness and that everyone was 'in this together' was a complete joke.

Equally nauseating for both Adrian and his brother was the frequent 'virtue signalling' by several public figures who not only seemed to relish the opportunity to do this, but somehow managed to raise this most insincere practice to something of an art form. It was a bit easier for his father living on the Dorset coast since he could go out for his usual enjoyable walks by the sea and harbour, though, rather strangely, he did seem far more worried about his own safety than one would have expected for a very trim and fit sixty-six-year-old man whom one would have fully expected to have been very mentally robust in the face of such a potential danger. Every time Adrian spoke with his father over the phone during this period, or communicated with him by email, Roger would talk about the great importance of his being very careful at all times. Adrian never quite understood his father's extreme concern about the need to be careful. An additional consequence of the pandemic was that Adrian had been so disillusioned and appalled at both what he saw on the hospital wards and the dreadful, indeed selfish and nasty, behaviour of some people in his city, that he immediately gave up clinical medicine and decided to become a full-time researcher, an area of scholarship for which as a young man he had already showed great aptitude. So, he reflects, one very bad thing led to something that turned out to be rather good. But for sure, 2020 was a terrible year for just about everyone, especially those who weren't wealthy.

As Adrian returned from his uncontrolled thoughts and to the reality of the day, he realised he still had a long way to go to get everything his father owned into some kind of order. He was just about to start filling up the eighth cardboard box of possessions to *'keep'* when he heard the soft chime of his mobile phone. He looked at his left wrist and lower forearm onto which was strapped the latest CONTO3/1 model, an updated version of the almost ubiquitous combined computer, mobile phone and

TV unit which had been generally available in most electrical hardware and IT shops for the previous six months. It strapped very snugly and comfortably onto the wrist and forearm and also had a small compartment to house the wearer's whole genome sequence which was recorded – all three billion base pairs of the DNA – onto a small disc which could be easily read by any competent doctor with the right equipment. The entire unit had only cost him £400 which was very cheap at the price and he'd had his genome sequenced for just £20 as it had become such an easy thing to do at that time. This information was almost compulsory to have to hand since preventative medicine had become so prominent. Adrian pressed a small button on the unit, moved his left arm near his mouth and started to speak to his brother whose facial image had appeared very clearly on the small screen in the centre of the unit.

'Ah Michael, it's good to hear from you.'

The voice that replies to him sounds remarkably clear, with no interference.

'Thanks Adrian, is everything OK there?'

'Yes, so far so good, but it's a hell of a sweat with all this stuff here.'

'I can imagine. I'm sure you're doing a great job of it.'

Adrian wipes his slightly moist brow with his free

right hand while speaking. 'Well I'm doing my best for sure… there's just so much stuff that Dad had here.'

'I can only imagine. He always was a bit of a hoarder, bless him.'

'Yes that's true but the problem is his books.'

'Books? What do you mean?'

'Hundreds of them. On every subject that you can imagine…'

'I can only imagine!'

'You know he was always a great reader. But he's even got a few books on supernatural events.'

'Well he was a polymath after all. He just wanted to know everything possible.'

Adrian sighs at this.

'Yes I guess that's it but the problem is where on earth are we going to put them all? And I really don't want to throw any of them away. That would be like sacrilege.'

'Yes,' replies Michael, 'that wouldn't be right. Anyway, I'm sure between the two of us we can accommodate most of them, the really good ones anyway.'

'Maybe we can donate the rubbish ones to charity.'

'Good thought brother. Bright chap.'

'So what time will you and Susan be coming down here tomorrow to help out?'

'I reckon about two in the afternoon at the latest, traffic permitting.'

Adrian relaxes a little when he hears this.

'OK that sounds good. Is there anything else you want me to do or look out for?'

'Yes, there's just one thing we need to check out.'

'And what's that?'

'Well, Adrian, do you remember those home movies that grandpa took of dad and his family – you know, the ones from when they were children which you very cleverly managed to combine into one big DVD from five old-fashioned cine reels?'

'Yes I do remember that. I gave it to dad over twenty years ago. But even if I manage to find it among this mess I don't think we'll manage to view it... I mean, DVDs of that time are obsolete aren't they?'

'Yes, true, but if you can also find dad's old DVD player then that might still work. Anyway, if the worst comes to the worst, I'm sure we can find some clever techno type person who'll be able to rescue the films and get it onto a disc we can see.'

'OK, I'll look for it carefully.'

'Try looking in the attic. Knowing dad, he may

have put it there.'

'Will do. But why would he put there?'

'Maybe he wanted to hide it for some reason.' Adrian thinks about this with just a hint of concern.

'Maybe.'

'Right. I'll see you tomorrow.'

'Good stuff. Bye Michael.'

The small screen showing his brother's friendly face suddenly faded into blackness and Adrian resumed his sorting and searching. But within a few minutes of this conversation, his curiosity got the better of him and he decided to rummage around his father's attic. He needed a small ladder to climb into the attic entry point which was just above the small study at the back of the cottage, and he soon found one in the corner of the garage which Roger must have used. He dragged the ladder inside, placed it below the attic opening and, climbing very carefully from the very top of the ladder, bundled himself into the attic space. Once inside, he was surprised to see how generous the available space appeared. At one of the corners of the low-ceilinged attic room he immediately saw two wooden boxes, one slightly larger than the other. He quickly made a beeline for the smaller of the two and rummaged around in its dusty contents. At the very bottom of the box he saw a large brown envelope with no markings from which he removed an old-fashioned DVD with the words 'family movie x 5' written in black with a felt pen on the upper surface. Delighted with this find he started the search for some kind of functioning DVD player in order to actually view what was on the disc.

Almost automatically, if not instinctively, he dragged the larger of the two boxes towards him and inspected the contents. It turned out there was only one object inside it which he guessed was a television with a built-in DVD player, an old model that was now obsolete but which might still work if he was lucky. Besides, he had no other options and his personal CONTO3/1 would certainly not be able to read the DVD. Thrilled with his unexpected find, he took two careful journeys to remove the television and the small player from the attic into the living room where he would be able, if he was very fortunate, to view its contents. The last time he'd seen this series of home movies was twenty-three years ago when he was just twenty-eight years old. He began to wonder if he had remembered all its contents.

By the time he'd placed the television onto the large wooden table in the living room and plugged it into the main electricity socket next to it, it was already late afternoon. While he felt hunger pangs, his inquisitive nature trumped his appetite for food. When he turned on the television he was both surprised and delighted to see that it was still working. They made them well in those days he thought. Nowadays everything electrical tends to break down. He took out the DVD home movie and carefully placed it into the player and waited to see what would happen, if anything.

First of all nothing, and then a jagged white flash that appears to enlarge and then rapidly contract holds his attention while he stares at the grainy and jerky images that begin to materialise before him. He'd already viewed the entire series of short films all rolled into one, but that was so very long ago that he had little recollection of the contents, although he knew they would trigger enjoyable memories of his father's past and act as a kind of historical record of life as it used to be in the middle of the previous century. He was enthused with anticipation and excitement even in his state of near exhaustion. But how much would he truly remember?

Almost immediately, the first reel shows him what he should have remembered and also what he would later try to forget. The sweeping views of the Swiss Alps came into view and showed him what an intrinsically gifted photographer his grandfather must have been with a keen aesthetic sense. Soon he sees the smiling and jerky images of his father as a rather self-conscious eight-year-old boy as well as his sister Margaret as a ten-year-old girl. How pretty a child she was, he thinks, and what a lovely aunt she would have made. Life is so cruel at times. That may be a truism, but he's never seen any reason to doubt it.

Then he sees it, or, more accurately, he sees him. His conscious brain and logical sense tries hard to deny what his eyes are telling him, but, in reality, seeing really is tantamount to believing, assuming it is not an optical illusion. But it isn't. Standing in the background of the scene, clearly visible a few yards behind the two children, is the clearest image possible of his father Roger. Neither of the children, nor their mother nearby, seems in the remotest bit aware of Roger's presence. His father looks exactly as he did when he first lived in Weymouth when he was sixty-three years old. It is a logical impossibility, but the evidence is staring at him. Roger glares intensely at the camera, not at the two children, and, remarkably, does not seem out of place which he should do. But casual clothing styles had changed little over the scores of years since the film was taken and his father seemed dressed more or less appropriately for the climate of Switzerland. Adrian watches the rest of the film in a sort of dazed state and appears to be mesmerised by what he sees. The film is both familiar and profoundly disturbing to him and throughout the whole film sequence, he sees his late father standing at some vantage point always behind everyone else, and with the same unchanging intense expression.

The obvious thing to do next was to watch the subsequent reels to see if the same thing might happen. The camera soon captures the tranquil torpor of the French Riviera, and this change of scene temporarily calms Adrian's mounting anxiety and sense of doom. But then he clearly sees his father again, dressed in the same short-sleeved shirt and light trousers, but this time he is engaged in what looks like a serious conversation with a twelve-year-old Margaret. Again, he knows this is logically and indeed temporally impossible, but here is the evidence literally staring him in the face. He moves his head from side to side in total disbelief and in the vain hope that this physical movement will in some way erase the disturbing images he sees on the screen. But, of course, the impossible images remain.

He has no option but to continue and by now he fully expects to see his father in film reels three, four and five. And, of course, he does. When he sees the grand ballroom reception in reel three, at first he only sees the usual suspects, including his father as a thirteen-year-old boy and his two grandparents greeting a vast number of relatives and friends. But just as he is starting to breathe a sigh of relief, he spots a grainy, but definite, picture of his father, again aged about sixty-three, and this time fully kitted out in a smart dinner suit, something he'd never seen him wear before or even possess. Roger seems to be trying hard to stay in the background of proceedings, but nevertheless he continues his intense glaring at the camera. The next shot is the most disturbing one as it shows with complete clarity what seems to be an intimate conversation between his father and the boy who is, of course, Roger as a younger person, the one who is being celebrated. The rest of the film is pretty routine stuff and very much as he remembers it. By the time the fourth reel started, Adrian was in a state of mild shock. The seemingly familiar sight of the pretty town of Davos in the Swiss Alps, and the slow sweeping views of the magnificent mountain scenery all around it, make him gasp with appreciation at nature's handiwork.

He was again struck by the quality of the camera work of his grandfather, but his father as an adult was absent during the first few minutes of the film. He saw the cable car slowly ascending the slopes of Mount Jacobshorn before he caught a quick glimpse of a boy of about fifteen, who was presumably the young version of his father, carefully walking upwards along a narrow gravel pathway to a viewpoint at the summit of the mountain. After a couple of minutes, he was joined by a man of medium height, wearing a thick grey coat and black gloves whom he immediately recognised as his father as an older man, again about the same age as he had appeared before. They seemed to have a brief conversation and then the film cuts out after exactly twenty minutes has elapsed. Adrian thinks he may as well look at the final reel though he dreads what it might show, as if he didn't know that. After the expected white and yellow flash, he sees before him a fine vista of some of the most beautiful Lakeland Fells, and these are all captured with the eye of a true photographer. The mountains are framed against a gentle backdrop of undulating green valleys while they are also framed elegantly below a tall blue sky with only an occasional wisp of white cloud. While admiring the sheer beauty of the Lake District, he is more than alarmed to see two figures slowly trekking up the arduous green slopes of Mount Skiddaw.

He knows that area of South Lakeland very well and recognises several key landmarks. But then the camera gradually hones in on the images of the two men and it is clear that one of them is his father, well kitted out for the trek but still clearly recognisable as the sixtyish man he knows so well, and the other is a good looking youth who is without any doubt a younger version of his father in a completely different age. They are both quite breathless judging by the way they are climbing, but they still appear to be having a serious conversation. This seems to last for rather longer than the previous ones he's seen on the other reels, and, just before the cine film terminates, the youth removes a piece of white paper from his left upper jacket pocket and gives it to his father. Roger as an adult looks at its written contents briefly, gives a knowing nod to the boy, and then says nothing further. The two of them are seen in the final shot to continue their slow ascent of the mountain.

A confused and stunned Adrian removes the DVD from the old player, places it carefully on the living room table, secretes himself into the one available armchair, and then starts to think about and try to make some sense of what he's just experienced. He is a serious and rational scientist without any belief in the supernatural, but here was cast iron proof of something he thought was just not possible in the real world. Meanwhile, he'd completely lost his appetite for dinner, and after about ten minutes he came to two conclusions. First, either he was mentally deranged or else he had just witnessed something bizarre but completely true. Second, and following on from the first conclusion, if these events portrayed in the films were true, then it was logical to assume that the implications of this had to be profound, and these were what frightened him most. So, he reasoned, God might well exist, supernatural events were a reality and not a product of our fears and imagination, time travel to the past and the future might be possible, imagining things strongly enough might influence reality, the list just went on. How would he explain this to his brother and also to his own wife Jacqui? She was a very sensible person, a real no-nonsense individual, and if she was also convinced by the films, then as far as he was concerned they were real. No question about it.

Anyway, he reckoned, as he was just about coming to terms with his new reality, his older lawyer brother and his wife would be joining him the next day, so he'll be able to show Michael and Susan all five reels and see what they have to say about the matter. Meanwhile, the one thing he just must do is have a really good night's sleep.

ABOUT THE AUTHOR

Peter Kennedy CBE, MD, PhD, DSc is a distinguished clinician and scientist who held the Burton Chair of Neurology for 29 years (1987-2016) at the University of Glasgow where he remains active in research and teaching as an Honorary Senior Research Fellow in the Institute of Infection, Immunity and Inflammation. He also has two Masters degrees in Philosophy, and has written five previous novels, an award winning popular science book on African Sleeping sickness, and co-edited two textbooks on neurological infections. He is a fellow of both the Royal Society of Edinburgh and the Academy of Medical Sciences.

BY THE SAME AUTHOR ALSO AVAILABLE ON AMAZON:

ARCADIAN MEMORIES AND OTHER POEMS (2020)

THE FATAL SLEEP (2019) - Luath Press, 3rd Edition

TWELVE MONTHS OF FREEDOM (2019)

CATAPULT IN TIME (2018)

RETURN OF THE CIRCLE (2017)

BROTHERS IN RETRIBUTION (2015)

REVERSAL OF DAVID (2014)

Printed in Great Britain
by Amazon